D1544159

SPICE

SPICE

JENNA JAMESON
and JAMIE K. SCHMIDT

Skyhorse Publishing

Copyright © 2014 by Jenna Jameson and Jamie K. Schmidt

All rights reserved. No part of this book may be reproduced in any manner
without the express written consent of the publisher, except in the case of
brief excerpts in critical reviews or articles. All inquiries should be addressed to
Skyhorse Publishing, 307 West 36th Street, 11th Floor, New York, NY 10018.

Skyhorse Publishing books may be purchased in bulk at special discounts for
sales promotion, corporate gifts, fund-raising, or educational purposes. Special
editions can also be created to specifications. For details, contact the Special Sales
Department, Skyhorse Publishing, 307 West 36th Street, 11th Floor, New York,
NY 10018 or info@skyhorsepublishing.com.

Skyhorse® and Skyhorse Publishing® are registered trademarks of Skyhorse
Publishing, Inc.®, a Delaware corporation.

Visit our website at www.skyhorsepublishing.com.

10 9 8 7 6 5 4 3 2 1

Library of Congress Cataloging-in-Publication Data is available on file.

Cover design by Brian Peterson
Cover photo credit: Thinkstock

Print ISBN: 978-1-62914-492-4
Ebook ISBN: 978-1-63220-132-4

Printed in the United States of America

Chapter One

Liz Carter knew all about feigning enthusiasm. She used to be the double-D diva "Spice," an international porn star and jet-setting party girl, after all. But after an unplanned pregnancy and nine years of raising her sweet little boy, it all seemed like a crazy erotic dream that had happened to someone else.

But faking orgasms was nothing compared to keeping her game face on while listening to this Common Core nonsense. She sat at a round chipped table in Jonathan's elementary school cafeteria during the monthly PTA meeting. The budget cuts were apparent in the shabby room. The setting sun cast a gloomy pall over the dirty, graffiti-stained walls. Shifting to get comfortable in the hard plastic chair, Liz looked around at the other parents. Some were listening intently to the droning voice of the principal, who bore a remarkable resemblance to Ben Stein in *Ferris Bueller's Day Off*.

Bueller? Bueller?

Others were texting or playing games on their phones. Was she the only one pissed off about this new school curriculum? While she agreed with the basic concept, Liz thought the rollout was a clusterfuck. Typos, directions written at a higher level than where the kids were reading, and incorrect answers were just the beginning of all that was wrong with the program.

When her third grader had said to her, "Mommy, I'm dumb. I don't get this. I hate school," that was the last straw.

Liz indicated to the moderator that she wanted to say something. When her turn came around, she wiped her sweaty palms on her Anne Klein thrift store-find pants. *No one was going to make her little boy feel stupid.*

"This came home the other day." Liz waved his homework sheet. "The math equation reads: $3 + 10 = 9 + 2$ and has two circles under the two for factoring. Thirteen doesn't equal eleven! Can we have a base for accuracy first, before we build on wrong information?"

The other parents murmured their agreement. Liz felt some of the tension ease from her shoulders. Maybe she wasn't going all "Tiger Mom" for nothing. The runner with the microphone brought the paper up to the principal, who squinted at the work. "Yes, your son should have put a one in each of the circles. Then draw a ten frame with nine dots colored in. One dot not colored in and then one dot on the outside of the box." He then beamed out at the crowd.

Liz wasn't the only one slack-jawed. The group of disgruntled parents waited for the principal to realize what he said had made no sense to the adults in the room, never mind the third graders. Closing her eyes, she tried to see it his way. She was reminded of the old joke, "I'm trying to see it from your point of view, but I can't get my head that far up my ass." Wiping the smirk off her face, she concentrated. It took a moment. She finally got the process, but didn't understand how it promoted learning. Opening her eyes, Liz continued. "I don't think you understand the frustration involved. My son knows his arithmetic. Up until this year, he loved school. These worksheets are counterintuitive, and they're making him dread going to class."

There was a splattering of applause that straightened Liz's spine. It was good to be in the spotlight again and even better to be wearing clothes. The principal harrumphed and went on about more parent training and how he stood by the curriculum and yadda, yadda, yadda.

I tried, baby.

Liz knew when to quit. She balled up the math paper when it came back to her and tossed it in the trash on her way out. If her cancer treatment hadn't knocked out most—*all*—of her savings, Liz would consider sending him to a private school. But she needed to start saving for college, now, if she wanted her nine-year-old to have a chance at higher education.

It was almost enough to consider going back into the business. Adjusting the strap on her plain white bra, Liz inwardly cringed. Even with the reconstructive surgery, her breasts wouldn't even get her a fluffer position in the industry—making sure the actors were-*ahem*-up for their scenes when needed.

Frankenboobs.

Her best friend, Sarah, smacked her when Liz told her what she thought of them. The scars were badges of honor, Sarah had said. She earned them through puking and persevering through the worst of the chemo.

"Liz, can I ask you something?"

Looking over her shoulder, she saw Damien's mother—what the hell was her name? Judith, Joy . . . crap. Liz plastered on an expectant smile but kept walking through the heavy double doors. Would this be the moment she got outed as a porn star? She had cut her hair and the double mastectomy had drastically reduced the size of her breasts, but she still feared that one day one of these urban Mommies would realize she used to fuck on camera and her son's life would change.

Judith/Joy caught up with her and matched her stride down the wide cement stairs. "I was wondering . . ."

Here it comes. Liz wondered how far she'd get on plausible deniability. She hadn't been a bad actress. Should she go for offended? *How dare you suggest such a thing? What kind of a pervert are you?* Maybe if she laughed it off? *Yeah, like I'm a porn star.*

"We need someone to do the flyers for the Halloween fundraiser. Chloe said you were the absolute best at this. Do you think you could help us out?"

"Of course." Relief shot through her and her knees wiggled a little. Liz wasn't even sure what she just agreed to, and who the hell was Chloe? Reaching into her bag, she pulled out her business card. LIZ CARTER GRAPHIC ARTIST. "Just email me the details."

"Fabulous," Joy/Judith gushed, and squeezed her arm before darting back into the school.

Liz blew out a deep breath. Her cover was safe. If it cost her a little extra time in Photoshop, it was well worth it. Between films, she had taken a slew of computer courses at UCLA, and it was the best thing she had ever done for herself. Her favorite had been learning the Adobe product line. She had lots of practice creating signs, business cards, and website banners for her fellow porn stars. Learning new skills kept her grounded when it seemed her only worth was how fast she could "make those jugs bounce," as one director said. It gave her the confidence that she could have a career that didn't involve anal sex.

But when she came back to New York, pregnant with Jonathan, Liz realized not only did she need another career, but she also needed a village to help raise her son. Or at the very least, some serious emotional support. Steve, Jonathan's father, didn't want the responsibility. Her brother in Kansas had all but written her off for her lifestyle choices, and even though the Bible said hate the sin, not the sinner, his zealot wife wouldn't allow her in their lives. Liz's mother had said she was too young to be a grandmother and that she'd done her bout as a mother and wasn't interested in another rug rat. Liz was on her own.

So she reached out to other men and women like her who were transitioning from adult entertainment back into the real world. The Internet was a wonderful place for making connections. And for every three mean trolls, one genuine person was looking for some comfort and support. From the early bulletin board forums to Facebook, Liz found her people, her village. Networking and going door-to-door to local businesses, she got her first few jobs as a freelance graphic designer. It took her a while to build a clientele, but she earned a reputation for coming through on last minute projects. It helped that being pregnant with Jonathan had made her so sick, she was up at all hours of the night.

But her little boy was worth it. He was the joy in her life. And she would do anything for him—including fighting pseudo-intellectuals who had their heads up their collective asses about education. After her cancer battle, the school district should be a cakewalk.

"I'll deal with it later," Liz thought, easing into the New York City sidewalk traffic like the native she was.

Her cancer was in remission and Jonathan was so damn smart, they'd get through this. She just hated disappointing him. Liz texted their downstairs neighbor Mrs. Ritter, who assured her that he was busy playing on the iPad Sarah and her husband, Cole, gave him for Christmas. Mrs. Ritter would soon put Jonathan to bed and then watch her shows on Liz's old TV.

"It's good you have a date," the sweet old woman had said as Liz kissed her son goodnight earlier that evening.

"It's not a date," Liz had laughed, squeezing in one last hug as Jonathan squirmed. "I'm going to yell at the school system and then I'm going out for coffee with a potential client."

That wasn't exactly the truth, but Mrs. Ritter would've had kittens if Liz told her she was meeting a former male stripper. But she had made a point to dress up more than she usually did. Money was tight and her clothes these days were more Walmart than Neiman

Marcus, which differed greatly compared to how she used to shop when she got a fat check from her producer. Before it was "let's hit the mall instead of doing laundry." Nowadays, she haunted thrift stores and street markets for vintage couture at a bargain price. Usually, she came up empty, but every now and then, she hit pay dirt. The outfit she was wearing today was a Chanel wool skirt that ended a little bit above her knees. Her blouse was a crisp pink Lands End cotton button down she bought at Sears on the clearance rack. Finishing off the outfit were her chocolate-colored knee-high boots, which she bought full price on Rodeo Drive during flusher times. Slipping her phone back in her pocket, Liz darted across the busy street before the WALK sign changed.

She was meeting Sean O'Malley at Nosh, one of her favorite neighborhood cafes. Sean, if he could be trusted, was looking for some help staying out of the business.

There wasn't a lot of support for former adult entertainers—even in Manhattan—so Liz made her own: FATE. Faith, Acceptance, Trust, and Enlightenment. In the beginning, she had spent a lot of time weeding out the wannabes and the pricks. Now, she maintained a private Facebook page that, while being members only, showed enough of FATE to attract like-minded people.

There was a genuine need to talk with someone who understood how hard it was to transition back to mainstream society. No one else could understand the temptations of quick and easy money versus holding yourself as worthy of a life that didn't revolve around being on your back. Liz learned the lesson long before she lost what her agent used to call her "money makers." And yet, on certain black days, she wondered if she'd ever be attractive to a man again. She was more than the sum of her bra size. Intellectually, she knew that. Sometimes she needed a reminder, though, and that's where FATE came in.

Liz had found a core group of friends in the support group she ran out of her apartment every Monday night. Peter, an ex-prostitute who now worked as a designer for Ralph Lauren, recently married the love of his life, Pol. Brian, a former videographer for a porn site, worked in a garage rebuilding classic cars. Honey, an Audrey Hepburn lookalike, was just starting her photography business and had found happily ever after with her husband, Marc.

At Honey and Marc's wedding, Jonathan had asked her, "When are you going to get married, Mom?" His sweet little boy question stabbed her in the heart.

"Well," Liz had said. "First, I have to get my Fairy Godmother to make me a dress."

"That's Sarah, right?" he had said.

Sarah, her best friend in the world, had also been a world famous porn star. "Sugar" had reinvented herself into a bestselling author and mom. Thanks to her marriage to millionaire Cole A. Canning, Sarah was taking Manhattan by storm.

If anyone fit the bill for Fairy Godmother, it was Sarah. As a matter of fact, Cole's charity sent Liz and Jonathan on an all-expense paid trip to Disney after she got through the cancer treatments and surgery. It had been a magical dream come true. She'd find a way to pay it forward. Someday.

"Then you have to go to the ball and meet Prince Charming," Jonathan had said, unwilling to let the subject drop, even when she had dragged him out on the dance floor.

"I'm not leaving a crystal Louboutin for him to find me," Liz had joked.

Not that she had any more. She sold the last pair on eBay a few months ago when it was time to go school shopping. It wasn't as though she needed a pair of sparkly sandals, but it had hurt all the same.

"No." Jonathan had shook his head with an earnestness that had melted her heart. "Just give him your cell phone number."

If it were only that easy, kid.

Liz got to the coffee house a few minutes early and snagged a booth in the corner. She liked being able to look over the menu. As a vegetarian, she was careful that what she ordered didn't have any animal products in it. She decided on a soy latte and a field green salad and opened her laptop while she waited for the waitress.

About three months ago, Sean O'Malley had sent her a private message wanting to learn more about FATE. They started out just conversing on Facebook and, once he gave her the name of the place he stripped at and his manager confirmed he worked there, Liz gave him her number and they started texting. Sometimes, it was just about silly stuff. Then they graduated to Skype. He was a good-looking guy and fun to talk to. Still, there was something niggling in the back of her mind that something about him was off.

Maybe she was just paranoid, but she kept getting the impression that he had to think too long about his answers. The delay went just a shade beyond being the introvert he claimed to be.

Introverted stripper. Liz snorted.

Scrolling through her emails, she re-read her favorites. Once, when he had been driving through Connecticut, he'd pulled over to take a picture of a highway sign. The sign was a typical "Welcome to name of town." In this case, the name of the town was Mianus.

Sean sent a picture of the sign WELCOME TO MIANUS and a text that said, "Traffic is really bad in Mianus."

For the rest of the day, they had played off that pun. Liz replied back, "I hate it when Mianus is backed up."

And it had devolved from there.

Aside from some bad puns, Sean was always respectful and polite. Any innuendos or crude jokes were harmless and generally self-effacing.

During a Skype session, his gaze never wandered from her face. So why hadn't she invited him to the Monday night group yet? Something just didn't jive. Did he do more than strip? It didn't matter to her if he sold his body, but that wasn't the vibe she was getting.

Everybody had secrets to hide and adult entertainers usually had more than most, hence the "a" for acceptance, but she had Jonathan to consider. The main reason she set up a face-to-face meeting was to see if the niggling doubt would go away. If Sean didn't earn her "t" for trust, he wasn't getting anywhere near FATE, her apartment, and her son.

"Thank God, it's Friday!"

Liz blinked up at the whoops and cheers. The businessmen at the next table should have been at a bar instead of a neighborhood joint like this. Liz tried to tune out their loud conversation, but when it turned ugly, she couldn't ignore it.

"Day-um, look at the fun bags on her."

For a moment, Liz bristled. And then she realized they weren't talking about her. While the reconstruction brought her down to a standard B-cup, they were nothing like her money makers had been. Men would walk into lamp posts when she passed them on the street wearing a V-neck sweater. Now, she barely got a double take. In fact, if she had her son with her, men generally avoided making eye contact.

"Do you think they're natural?"

"Who cares?"

"I think she's going to pop a button."

"I'm popping something."

The poor woman in question was their waitress who, judging by her set jaw, heard every word. "Have you decided?" The waitress asked her, blinking back tears.

Liz placed her order. She had skipped lunch and it was well past dinner. Sean O'Malley was late, and if he was planning on blowing her off, she was going to take advantage of an opportunity for a peaceful meal—one that didn't involve negotiations about eating the final bites of broccoli.

The men at the table sniggered as the waitress turned to go back into the kitchen.

"I'd die happy, suffocated by those."

So much for peaceful.

If Jonathan were there, she wouldn't make a scene. She'd quietly tell her son that gentlemen didn't comment on a lady's appearance, but not everyone was raised well enough to learn that. But Jonathan wasn't here, and Liz was damned if she was going to huddle in silence while this poor girl was forced by her job to be polite.

"Excuse me," Liz said, raising her voice to be heard over their frat boy antics.

"Are you talking to me?" the ringleader said. He was slick, from the top of his perfectly coiffed hair to his pristine wing tips. Handsome in a trust fund metrosexual way, he oozed entitlement. His merry men were cut of the same cloth, but they reeked of desperation. Desperate to fit in. Desperate to make their sales quota. Desperate for sex.

"Yeah, look, I know what I'm about to say isn't going to bring you clarity, but would you want someone to talk about your daughter, your mother, your wife like that?" Liz made an effort to sound reasonable and non-threatening.

"My wife ain't stacked like that." He flashed his teeth at her. They were so white, she was momentarily distracted by the gleam.

"What would she think, you talking about another woman like that?"

"She ain't here."

He smacked high fives with his friends.

"You're being obnoxious," Liz said. "And it's a free world, but you're making me and probably a few other women really uncomfortable. Is that what you want?"

"Why don't you mind your own business?"

"I'd love to," she said, sincerely. "But you've got volume control issues." Liz made a "turn down" gesture with her hands.

"Are you one of those Femi-Nazis?"

Liz wished she had a bingo card. She could put a marker on the Femi-Nazi square. It was right next to the "Are you a Lesbo?" and "You're just jealous."

"Heil Steinem," Liz said, shooting her arm straight out. A little levity never hurt any situation, right?

"Look, lady, we're just trying to blow off steam and have a little fun," said a tired looking man with a rumpled tie and disheveled hair. He held on to his coffee cup like it was her AVN award for best blow job. "Lighten up. Life doesn't have to be so serious."

Liz mentally marked off another two bingo squares. "I get that. But it's at the expense of another person. You're being a bully."

They rolled their eyes almost in unison, and Liz knew she was wasting her time.

"We're complimenting her," Ringleader piped up. "She's gorgeous. She could be a model. That's the problem with chicks today. They can't take a compliment."

Another bingo square marked off. "Okay, I'm giving you the benefit of the doubt that you're not actively being demeaning with the whole 'chick' thing. 'Fun bags' also isn't a compliment."

"How about 'nice tits'?" Ringleader leered at her.

For a moment, Liz was taken aback. Part of her wanted to lift up her shirt and show him the scars that crisscrossed her breasts.

Still think they're nice?

But with her luck, she'd probably get arrested for indecent exposure.

"How about 'nice eyes'?" she countered.

"I'm not interested in her big . . . *eyes*. Why are you so uptight? Is she your girlfriend?"

Liz mentally drew a line over her imaginary bingo card. *BINGO.* Not because he was right, but because he and his buddies had used every nasty excuse and innuendo she'd heard time and time again.

"That's enough, needle dick."

Surprisingly enough, the comment didn't come from the waitress and it was too deep of a voice to have slipped out of Liz's mouth. The table of cretins joined her in gaping at the newcomer. Had there been a trace of Ireland in that sneering sentence?

Well, hello Sean O'Malley. Better late than never.

Liz's eyes travelled over his large, muscular frame. Skype hadn't done him justice. He was tall so she had a ways to look up. His narrowed hazel eyes focused in on the suits at the other table like he was ready to rip them apart. Shaggy black hair framed the now familiar face, which had probably been heartbreakingly pretty about ten years ago, but had matured into rugged good looks. Up close and in the fading daylight, Liz now saw his nose had been broken and badly set, throwing off the perfection of his high cheekbones and stubborn jaw. Life had shaped his face with character-building creases around his mouth and eyes. She liked to think they were smile lines, but he was glowering too fiercely at the men to be sure.

In the bad lighting and webcam pixels, he hadn't been coiled to strike like a jungle cat. Swallowing to ease her dry throat, she admired how he held the attention of the businessmen, who looked away one at a time until it was just Ringleader holding his gaze.

He didn't act like the dancers she knew or the men on the porn sets. They wouldn't risk a fight that would put a bruise on their bodies—or worse, injure them. Sean didn't seem to care. Was that what was bothering her about his story? She glanced down at his knuckles when he clenched his hands. The first two knuckles were callused, as though he made a living using his fists.

Liz frowned. When they had Skyped, he seemed more of a lover instead of a fighter. But he balanced himself on the balls of his feet like he was ready to take on all comers. Strippers didn't usually beat up people. But, Liz had checked up on his story and he had been telling the truth. Sean had been a dancer at Club 69 on the Upper East Side. His boss had missed him. Wanted to know when he'd be back. Said he was quite a draw.

Quite indeed.

He wore a gray hoodie half-zipped over a tight, white T-shirt and his jeans were snug enough she could see why he was so popular.

Oh my.

Liz moved her gaze down his muscled thighs. Her own thighs quivered and she glanced back up. He had caught her looking. There was enough steam in his gaze to make her giddy before he returned to glaring at Ringleader.

This is new.

She'd practically lived as a monk these past nine years and hadn't missed sex. Liz had begun to think that she fucked so much on camera, she used up her quota in this lifetime. Well, that wasn't entirely true. Sometimes she also missed the intimacy that came after a good romp in the sack, the cuddling, and the sweetness of waking up in someone's arms. However, it also took a lot of energy trying to figure out who wanted to date Liz and who wanted to fuck "Spice"—energy she couldn't spare between raising her son and her business. She took the edge off with an active fantasy life and a slew of battery operated gadgets, but with her life with Jonathan to consider, no one she met ever interested her enough to take home. Was she thinking about taking Sean O'Malley home?

Liz shook her head. *No.* Only as a new FATE member and only if she could get rid of the feeling that he was hiding something.

"Let's get out of here," Ringleader said, finally dropping his gaze. He threw a hundred-dollar bill down on the table.

Liz sincerely hoped that covered the tip, as well. She'd hate to think her big mouth stiffed the waitress. Sean waited until all the men left, staring bullet holes in them. Then he sank into the booth.

"Troublemaker, huh?" he said, a faint Irish brogue making her panties a little damp.

"They weren't so tough." Liz dismissed the suits with a wave of her hand.

"I was talking about you."

"Me?" Liz reared back. "What do you mean?"

"I mean, a woman with any sense doesn't start a fight with five men."

"We're in a crowded restaurant."

"Right now you are. What happens when you go to leave and they're waiting in the alley for you?"

Liz flushed. "I appreciate your concern, but that wasn't going to happen. They're businessmen in suits, not gang members."

"Don't be so fucking naive."

Was it wrong that the way he said *fucking seriously turned her on*? "I didn't invite you here for a lecture," she told him primly, while she looked back to her laptop. Maybe she left her composure on the screen?

The waitress brought over her latte and salad. "Something for you?" she asked Sean, all business.

"Coffee, black. And one of those cinnamon buns."

"You got it," the waitress said. "And thanks, both of you, for what you said."

"Anyone would have spoken up," Liz said. But they both knew that wasn't true.

"I still appreciate it."

When the waitress walked away, Sean shrugged off his hoodie. Liz nearly snorted her latte. Wow. If she'd had a doubt he was a stripper, the casual, sensual way he shed his coat would have convinced her.

Eyes up there. She forced herself to stop ogling his cut biceps.

He'd caught her again. There was a sparkling warmth in his eyes she was trying not to find enchanting.

Business. He obviously wasn't looking for a date. He needed FATE and her support, not another screaming groupie who wanted his body.

Chapter Two

Sean O'Malley hadn't expected to feel anything but satisfaction and maybe a surge of lust when he met with Spice, a.k.a Liz Carter. In person, she didn't disappoint. Beautiful, luscious, her wide, full mouth was made for kissing and he knew the full extent of what she could do with it. He had a few of her movies downloaded on his laptop.

The whole protective thing that jolted through him had caught him by surprise. When he walked in and she was facing down five men who looked like they were drawing straws to see who got to hold her down and fuck her first, his temper ignited.

It lowered to a slow burn when she stared at him with those deep brown eyes, giving him the once over like he was on stage. Well, that was his cover, wasn't it? She wouldn't be sitting next to him now if she knew he was just using her for his research paper about the adult entertainment industry.

Think of Mary Katherine.

But he didn't want to think about his sister right now. For the first time in a long time, Sean wanted to put aside his data points and hypothesis and share a cup of coffee with a gorgeous woman with wavy black hair through which he was dying to run his fingers.

"I'm glad we were able to finally meet in person," Liz said, attacking her salad with a vengeance.

His sister used to do that, like all that rabbit food was the best thing she ever tasted. It had to be farm grown or organic or free range. Sean stared down into his coffee. He supposed the meth had been home grown.

"Earth to Sean." She snapped her fingers.

"Sorry," he said, rubbing his face. "Long day."

"Tell me about it. Sometimes it helps to have a friendly ear."

He wished he could, but it would skewer his data. "You know how it is. Sometimes you're the windshield, sometimes you're the *hemipteran.*"

"The what?" Liz asked, forkful of mesclun paused by her mouth.

"Sorry, just channeling my inner Sheldon Cooper. Bug." Sean made squishing sounds.

"Who squished you today?"

"Who didn't," he countered. "It doesn't matter. I don't want to think about the exterminators. I want to get to know you better."

Liz finished her salad and cupped her hands around her latte. "I'm a what-you-see-is-what-you-get type of person. What do you want to know?"

Now was his chance. If only he had his laptop—anything to record her next few words. But how was he going to ask his most important question without sounding like a tabloid reporter?

"What's your favorite color?" he blurted out.

"Seriously, O'Malley?"

"I panicked," he admitted. "I went with the safe question."

"Blue," she said. "You going to share that?" Liz nodded to the cinnamon bun.

Sean broke off a piece and handed it to her. He liked the way her eyes tracked his tongue as he licked the icing off his finger. Indulged himself in how it would taste licking it off her body. To his surprise, she blushed and looked away.

A blushing porn star. What were the odds?

"How's school going?" she asked, fiddling with her fork.

For a moment, he blanked, trying to remember his story. Oh yeah, Sean took a deep breath. He hated lying. His cover was that he went back to school as an undergraduate at NYU and started to strip to pay his way through college. Not very original, but it worked. In truth, when he wasn't teaching, his day job was at a juvenile clinic for troubled youth. Although, he did spend a week stripping at Club 69 so he wasn't totally full of shit.

"Good. I like my classes." Or rather, he liked those classes when he took them six years ago. Now, he taught them. He had a BS and a masters in social work. Being a teaching assistant helped keep his tuition bills down while he went for his PhD.

However, even before that, he had been the biggest nerd in high school. He graduated two years early. Other kids dreamed of being pro ballers and rock stars. Sean wanted to be a cultural anthropologist. No posters of Kobe Bryant and Shaq on his walls. He would have plastered his room with James Clifford or George Marcus, but, sadly, they don't make trading cards of ethnographic authorities. It was a good thing his father made him take boxing lessons, or he would've been the poster child for Swirly Qs.

"I was an English lit major," Liz said, taking another piece of his cinnamon bun.

Sean choked down a laugh, but didn't conceal his grin in time. "What?"

"Nothing," he shrugged.

Liz's eyes narrowed on him. "Go ahead. Say it."

Now he was the one blushing. "I don't know how without sounding like an asshole."

A smile twitched on her face. She was lovely, and she made him feel a little goofy when he looked at her too long. "Let me guess," Liz drawled. "You've seen *A Sale of Two Titties*?"

"I might have," he hedged, the burn on his cheeks something he wished he could will away.

"Did you know we were threatened with a lawsuit over the title?"

"There was another porn movie featuring Charles *Dick-ins*?" Sean was trying not to picture her doing a reverse cowgirl on some faceless stiff, her naked body facing the camera as she bounced up and down. It was bad enough his cock was pressing at the seams of his jeans just from being near her. She oozed sensuality. He hadn't been prepared for that. In their emails and texts, she seemed more like the girl next door. The rapport they shared made it easy to forget who she used to be and why he was here.

"It's actually taken from a Monty Python skit," she said.

"My mind is going places it shouldn't, thanks to the python imagery," he admitted.

Her laugh trilled across the cafe, attracting interested male attention. He glared them down.

"Why do you do that?" she asked.

"What?"

"Scowl like that. They're just looking to see what all the hubbub is about."

"Maybe," Sean said, still eyeballing a clueless hipster. "But then they're noticing what a beautiful woman you are."

When she didn't say anything, he brought his attention back to her. She was shredding the napkin. "Why do you care?"

"I don't know," he said honestly. He held out his hand and she laid hers inside it. Rubbing his thumb across her knuckles, Sean watched as Liz took a trembling breath. "Does it make you uncomfortable that I've seen your movies?"

"A bit, but probably not for reasons you think." She moved her leg under the table so it brushed his.

"Tell me." He told himself this connection was just that he was getting closer to understanding what happened to Mary Katherine. To do that, he needed to get into the FATE group. He should have his "eyes on the prize" as his sparring partner, McManus, always said. He'd be busting a nut if he could see Sean now.

"I don't mind that you watched my movies," Liz said, breaking into his thoughts.

"You don't?"

"Did you get off?"

Sean was glad he didn't have a mouthful of coffee. He'd have spit it out all over the table. "Yeah."

Liz nodded. "That's the point of the movie. If there weren't any buyers, there wouldn't be any movies. So you've seen me fuck. I know you jerked off to it. No embarrassment. It is what it is."

His dick lurched when she said *fuck*. God, he wanted to kiss her.

"So what makes you uncomfortable?" he asked.

She took a few deep breaths, started to say something, and then looked away.

"I'm not judging you," he said to fill the silence. "I don't understand the whys, though. Why a girl gets into porn. But I'd like to know." His hand tightened on hers. It surprised him that it wasn't just the scientist in him talking. He really wanted to hear her answer.

"You want to know why I got started in porn?" She seemed relieved to be asked that question. They had kept their conversations to safe topics when they were exchanging those first few texts and Skype, feeling each other out, making sure the other wasn't a psycho. Tonight was more intimate and it was so unlike what he expected, Sean felt that he was three steps behind. He hadn't expected the sizzle between them.

"Sure, as long as it doesn't make you uncomfortable to tell me."

"I wanted to." She sent him a challenging look

"You wanted to?" Sean was about to burst out of his jeans.

"I love sex."

She's trying to kill me.

"I was offered a lot of money."

He managed a nod.

"And I was good at it."

He nodded again before he caught himself.

"But that's over now. Just like you're not stripping anymore, right?"

Clearing his throat, Sean said, "Right." It was bad enough working a full shift at the clinic and then almost pulling an all-nighter dancing for horny chicks with dollar bills. His schedule was brutal. Monday, Wednesdays and Fridays at the clinic and Tuesdays and Thursdays at the college. Sometimes he double dipped and did both jobs every day, and if he was backlogged, he worked weekends. Although, his weekends were usually booked for his ethnography project, which he would eventually expand into his thesis. Which reminded him, he should go to campus and check on his algorithms.

Sean shook his head. No time to think about that now. She didn't know how busy he was. Maybe she thought he was stripping again. Sean stifled a snort. He had barely lasted the week. It had been for research and for Mary Katherine. He couldn't see himself stripping long term.

"Do you miss it?"

"No," he said. "It was exciting at first. Having the women scream at me. Jam fives and tens down my pants. You wouldn't believe the offers I got."

Liz raised an eyebrow.

"Well, maybe you would," Sean said. "I got jaded too fast and it wasn't fun anymore. The money was still good." And it had been. He managed to pay a few bills. "But I didn't like the contempt that was under the admiration." And he didn't like the assumption he would fuck anyone for the right price. "One woman, attractive, in her mid-fifties, wouldn't take no for an answer. She paid the hundred dollars to be in the VIP room and wanted me to go down on her. Starting bidding on it. She was up to five thousand dollars before I left the room. I was a dancer, not a gigolo, but she didn't seem to care or think there was a difference. I didn't go back after that."

"Were you afraid she was going to stalk you?" Now it was her turn to give his hand a comforting squeeze.

"Not really. I figured if it wasn't her, it would only be a matter of time before it happened again."

"Why didn't you take the cash? That's a lot of money for a half hour's work."

"Would you have done it?" he asked.

"I've done girl-on-girl scenes."

Dear God, his heart just stopped.

"It's just body parts. Don't get me wrong, I prefer men. You told me you got into stripping for the tips. That five grand was more than you made in a weekend, right?"

"Yeah, but—"

"You don't like licking pussy?" Liz asked him, batting her eyelashes at him.

Had all the air suddenly been sucked from the room?

"I uh—"

"I'm just messing with you," she said. "But not everyone would have walked away from getting paid for doing something they liked to do. Would you have changed your mind if it was a hot young chick?"

"No."

"Why?"

"Because I'm not for sale."

"What if you needed the money for something?"

"I'd go without."

"What if it was for an operation?" She pressed on.

"This is like the old Winston Churchill line."

"Huh?" Liz cocked her head to the side.

"Churchill asked a woman if she'd sleep with him for five million pounds, and after hemming and hawing, she agreed. Then he asked her if she'd sleep with him for five pounds. And she said, 'Of course not, what do you take me for?' And he said, 'We've already established that. Now we're negotiating price.'"

Liz slowly clapped her hands. "Cute story. But you know it's not always so cut and dry. You were tempted, weren't you?"

"No." He shook his head.

"I can't tell if you're lying to me or not."

"Would you give a guy a blow job for five thousand dollars?" he scoffed.

Liz considered it. "Cash?"

"Sure," he croaked.

"No, but I would be tempted."

Sean ran a hand over his face. She was so matter-of-fact about it. "Why would you say no, then?"

"Because it's a slippery slope. If you give in this time, you'll probably give in next time."

Sean's fingers itched for his keyboard. Now, they were getting somewhere. "So being in adult entertainment is like an addiction?"

Her laugh trilled out again, and he couldn't take his eyes off her to stare down anyone. "In some cases, yes. There's an interesting power dynamic. You must have felt it up on stage."

He had. When he was dancing, the energy was like an adrenaline rush and a turn on. He did have power to make women cream their panties just by showing them his dick.

"So I'm wondering," Liz said, leaning in across the table, "if the real reason you turned down that money was because once you crossed that particular line, it would have opened up a door that you didn't want open."

"That's very deep," he said. "Are you sure you weren't a psych major?"

"'Sometimes a cigar is just a cigar.'"

She quoted Freud to him. He felt like Gomez Addams. *Tish, you spoke French.* He could talk to her all night. But she must have sensed the evening was getting off track because she leaned back in her chair and the moment of intimacy was broken when she brought up the main reason they were here tonight.

"I think you'd like our group. FATE."

Yes! He was in.

"So do I pass muster?" he asked, just to be sure.

"I haven't decided yet," she told him.

Crap. How many more hoops was he going to have to jump through?

But he liked her honesty, even if it pissed him off. "Why?"

She lifted a slim shoulder. "Intuition."

Sean knew she wasn't a flighty airhead and that he was a bad liar. He should take this as a sign to get out now. He could walk away and find more dancers to interview, maybe take a few prostitutes out to dinner and see if he could gain something tangible, something quantitative. Find some explanation so he could stop this obsessive need to understand and just get on with his life.

"I'm not sure what more you want from me," he said.

"To be honest, I don't know myself. Are you playing me for a fool? Or have you been totally honest with me?"

Sean wanted to come clean. It started out as a unique research opportunity. There weren't many places to observe retired adult entertainers. He tried his hand at stripping, but it didn't provide any lightbulb moments. The cash was great. The people, for the most part, decent.

So how did Liz manage to escape the life when his sister couldn't? He owed it to his parents to find out.

The waitress dropped off the check while he searched Liz's eyes to see how much she trusted him. She wanted to believe him. It felt dirty to lie to her. He let go of Liz's hand. But he was going to do it anyway. How would he react if this was all real and she didn't believe him? His pride would make him walk away.

Take a risk. The worse that can happen is she lets you go.

A part of him wanted that, wanted to put this all behind him and spend his nights with a super computer doing endless "what if" scenarios. But another part of him wanted her too much for this to be the last time they connected.

"I was a stripper. Now I'm not," he said and held her gaze. "If you don't want me in your little group, just say so."

"What are you so angry about?"

He was never very good at hiding his feelings. The best lie was sheathed in truth. "My sister." He drained his coffee in one gulp. "This was a mistake. Sorry for wasting your time."

Sean got up from the table. It was for the best. Liz was too distracting. He liked talking with her, wanted to do more than talk. The deception made him feel sleazy.

"Wait," she said, catching up to him as he was settling the check. "If it was just me, I wouldn't be so cautious. But there are other people to worry about."

"Why?" Sean signed the credit card receipt, waving away her attempt to reimburse him.

"Because they have lives and loved ones they want to protect from that contempt you were just talking about."

"No," he said, leaning down so his face was close to hers. He wanted to kiss her until they were both breathless. "Why, if it was only you, wouldn't you be so cautious?"

Flustered, she pushed him back. "Because I'm not ashamed of what I've done. I made my choices and I stand by them. I'll defend my actions and not give a shit what anyone else thinks. Others are not so lucky. Innocents could be hurt. I'm not taking that risk without good reason." Liz reached out to touch his arm. "I think you'd get a lot out of our FATE group. But I need a little more time to make sure you're a fit for us. I want to get to know you better. Can you understand that?"

"I have another problem," Sean said, walking with her toward the door.

It was a beautiful night. The city was buzzing, getting ready for the nightlife. But for the moment, everything was still and peaceful.

"What?" Liz asked.

"I want you."

He pulled her in close, giving her time to stop him if she wanted to. Sean let her feel how hard she made him, saw the haze of desire cloud her eyes before they half closed. Her lips tasted like cinnamon and sweet icing when he covered his mouth over hers. She stood on tiptoes to deepen the kiss and he wrapped her arms around her. When she snuggled tight against him, he could explore the curves of her back. The little moan she made as their hips rubbed together pleased him on a primitive level. Gripping her hair, he kissed her harder.

"Get a room," some asshole snarled.

Sean released her as she stepped away, but didn't go after the guy when Liz laid her hand on his arm.

"You solve a lot of your problems with your fists?" she asked, holding his hand in hers. She rubbed her thumb across the calluses on his knuckles.

"Sometimes."

"Dangerous pastime."

"You want to get to know me?" He slung an arm around her shoulders.

"Sure," she said.

"Got some time?"

"For what?"

"I want to show you where I spend my free time."

"Okay," Liz said, and after a few moments slid her arm around his waist as he signaled for a taxi.

Chapter Three

Liz sat in the cab, aware of the big male body next to her. It was inappropriate for her to be fantasizing about kissing him again, especially if she was serious about making sure he wouldn't blab FATE's secrets to the world. She didn't want to be distracted by his hard physique and killer smile. Liz wanted to make a calm, rational, decision.

And then go back to living like a nun.

She had a terrible suspicion there would be no going back after that kiss. What the hell was she going to do if he tried to touch her breasts? She could lie and tell him she got a breast reduction, but then there was the little fact that she had no sensitivity in them anymore. Sitting so close to him, Liz realized she wanted his hands on her body.

He wanted her.

She was more stunned by that statement than she was by the kiss, which nearly short-circuited her brain. All that chatting over Skype and the emails and texts they exchanged over the past few weeks had been foreplay, and she hadn't realized it until now.

Checking her phone, she realized she would have to relieve Mrs. Ritter in about two hours. That wasn't enough time for a first time. Was she actually considering sleeping with Sean O'Malley? Liz studied his profile in the cab, his five o'clock shadow stubble on his face. She imagined how it would feel against her inner thighs. Yeah, more than considering it. What would her friends say?

Sarah and Peter would cheer. Holly would say it was about time. Brian would say, cool. And Jonathan? Well, Jonathan didn't have to know yet. Maybe would never know. Liz bit her lip and wondered if she was doing the right thing.

The taxi stopped and Sean paid the driver while she got out of the car. They were in front of a building called McManus's Place.

"Is this a bar?" she asked.

"Not exactly," Sean said, taking her elbow and guiding her inside.

The smell hit her almost as soon as the sounds of men punching each other did. It was a gym. And while it smelled like sweat and old gym socks, it looked clean and orderly.

"You're here late, O'Malley," a big man with no neck said. He came up to them and clapped a meaty hand on Sean's shoulder.

"I'm showing my girl around," Sean said. "Sp—Liz, this is McManus. He owns the joint."

Liz bristled at the near slip. He still thought of her as Spice. She was just a porn star fantasy to him. She should have known better.

"What on Earth are you doing with a punk like this one?" McManus said to her, taking her hand and kissing it like she was Queen of the Bronx.

"I'm beginning to ask myself the same question," Liz said, ignoring Sean's dark look.

"Smart girl," McManus grunted. "So are you going to get in the ring and try to impress the lady?" he said to Sean.

"I hadn't planned on it."

"That's not necessary," Liz said. "I actually have to be going soon."

"I want to show you something," Sean said.

"It was nice meeting you," she said to McManus as Sean pretty much dragged her toward two swinging doors.

"What's the matter?" he asked when they passed through into a hallway.

"You. My name is Liz." She lowered her voice. "Don't you ever call me Spice, ever again. It's shit like that—" she punctuated each word with a sharp jab of her finger into his chest. "—that makes me leery about having you meet the members of FATE."

"I'm sorry," Sean said, stopping in the hall to face her. "It won't happen again."

Liz tried to hold on to her anger, but in the face of his sincerity, it slipped away. She gave him a tight nod. "So what do you want to show me?" she asked grudgingly. If he thought he was going to get a little action in the locker room, he had another think coming.

"I want to show you the youth boxing league I set up." Sean led her a room that opened up into a gymnasium. Liz marveled at the new equipment.

"How did you do all this?" She walked into the gym, touching the jump ropes and boxing gloves.

"McManus wrote a grant and several foundations either donated the goods or gave us the money to implement the programs. I teach three after-school sessions a week, focusing on fitness and self-defense."

Liz crinkled her nose. "Do you have to teach fighting?"

"About half my class are girls afraid to walk home alone."

"Oh." Now, she felt about as big as a thimble. She'd just assumed they were gang members getting off on beating the crap out of each other. "This is really great. It brings the community together."

"Exactly. It gives the kids a place to go. We're concentrating on physical activity and personal safety. It beats having them play on their phones all afternoon."

"Why are you showing me this?" she asked.

"McManus would say it's because I was trying to brag or get into your pants."

"Are you?"

"No, to the first. Yes, to the second, but not because of what is in this gym."

Liz felt a flutter in places that hadn't fluttered without battery operated assistance in a long time.

"I brought you here to show you that I have roots. I've got kids that depend on me. I have responsibilities. Sure, I've got a temper and yes, I get in the boxing ring and work that out. But I'd never put you or your friends in harm's way. I understand if you don't want a guy like me in your group. I'm not glamorous or well known. I'm just a schlub that bared his ass for a while."

"It's not that," she said. *This was all wrong.* "I don't want to exclude anyone from getting the understanding and support they need. You said in your emails you just wanted people to talk things over with, to feel that you weren't so alone. I'm not going to shut you out. I need you to meet the rest of the group. If they like you as much as I like you, then you're in."

"You like me?"

Liz nodded.

"When can I see you again?"

"I'll have to check with the other FATE members' schedules—"

"Not them, you, just you. I want to see you again, soon."

"How about this weekend?" Liz thought fast. Sarah and Cole offered to take Jonathan to the park for a few hours so she could finish up some design work in peace. But hell, she could work some long nights.

"Sure, you want to go to Washington Square Park? We could have a picnic."

"I'd like that."

"It's a date then."

A date. The first one she'd had in about ten years. What the hell was she getting into?

✳✳✳ ✳✳✳

What the hell am I getting into?

Sean saw Liz into a cab and went back into the gym. He didn't have time for a relationship. He couldn't get involved with Liz, not when he was pretty much trying to use her and her friends to provide research for a possible dissertation topic. It wasn't that he didn't try to do it above board, but no one credible would talk to him. Fuck him? Sure, that wasn't a problem as long as his credit card was good—not that he ever took them up on it. But every time he tried to ask what got them into the business, he got a boatload of crap designed to make the buyer feel better.

I'm paying my way through college.

My son's private school bills are too much for me.

I really like meeting new people.

I love sex.

Sean swallowed hard, seeing Liz's face when she said it to him.

Mary Katherine didn't get involved in porn for any of those reasons—unless it was the last one, and Sean wasn't quite ready to think about that yet.

"Get in the ring," McManus sighed. "You're thinking too much, *Perfessor*." McManus sneered the last word.

Sean nodded. He needed to burn off the self-recriminations and the angsty feelings brought on by thinking about Mary Katherine. Hitting the locker room, he shucked off his clothes and got into his training gear. Grimacing at his reflection in the mirror, Sean popped in his mouthguard. He didn't look like a teaching assistant working on his doctorate or even a counselor; he looked like a thug who used to strip for a living. So why wasn't Liz buying his spiel?

Because you're full of shit.

Sean figured Liz accepted his picnic invitation because it gave her another chance to check him out to see if he was right for the group. If he was lucky, she'd tell him what he needed to know and he could put all this lying and pretending aside. Would she even be interested in him if he wasn't looking to get into FATE? How much of that kiss was him and how much of it had been her? He left the locker room, shaking his head at his distracting thoughts. He needed to get his mind settled for the sparring match McManus set up, probably against Kyle Donovan.

Donovan was trying to decide whether to go MMA or stick to boxing. In either event, he hit like a wrecking ball and was a fast little ferret who preferred to work on the body. Sean would take the bruises on his ribs as a penance for lying to Liz. And for failing Mary Katherine.

So why did Liz kiss him back?

McManus tied up his gloves and slapped him on the ass. Ducking into the ring, Sean shook out his arms and his legs. He should have warmed up a bit. He was a little relieved to see that instead of Donovan one of McManus's newer guys was climbing into the ring. Sean could let his mind wander a bit while his body went through the movements.

They touched gloves, and the kid lunged with a wild haymaker. Sean veered and danced away, shooting McManus a *"really?"* look. McManus's snort sounded a lot like a laugh. The kid, who was more muscle than brains, put his head down and charged. Sean swatted him in the side of the head, lazily like a mother bear disciplining her cub.

"Hands up, Meat," Sean growled at the kid.

The kid threw a jab. Sean's brain clicked into analysis mode. Time slowed down as he watched the jab unfold: Shoulder flexion. Inward rotation of the arm at the glenohumeral joint. Slight horizontal adduction at the shoulder. Elbow extension. Wrist flexion. Pronation as the kid's foot rolled inward. Sean's body registered the impact of the punch, but he shrugged it off. Encouraged, the kid threw another jab. Sean leaned to avoid it and let a right cross fly into the kid's face. The kid staggered back, shaking his head from the tag.

"Is this a tea party?" McManus shouted. "Knock his head off."

Not sure who he was talking to, Sean kept in close and exchanged a few more blows with the kid, who had some raw power, but no control.

"It's like watching *Swan* fucking *Lake*. Come on, ladies, before I get out the tutus."

Sean landed another punch that rocked the kid's head back. The kid recovered and sent a flurry of jabs into Sean's sides. While mostly blocking them with his elbows, Sean still grunted at the impact. The kid was aggressive and hungry, but would need a lot more work on tactics. The only punch in his arsenal seemed to be the jab.

Swinging into a brutal upper cut that went mostly unchecked, Sean showed the kid how to follow through with a relentless series of blows, peppering the kid's weak defense. Losing himself in rhythm, Sean's mind finally cleared and hit a peaceful zone where without any incriminating thoughts. No guilt, just the sheer drive of adrenaline.

"That's enough," McManus called, ending the match.

Sean had trapped the kid in the corner. Backing off, Sean nodded at him. "Not bad, kid. You can take a pummeling, that's for sure."

The kid gulped air, his hands on his knees. "Thanks."

"Brody, my grandmother could have done better than that," McManus snarled.

"Don't let him get to you," Sean said in a low voice. "His granny's a tough broad."

Brody choked on a laugh.

"Hit the showers, kid." The disgust dripping from McManus's voice could sand blast the graffiti off the gym's doors. "And you," he turned his bile-infested gaze to Sean, "could actually make a career out of this if you didn't have your goddamned head in the clouds."

One of the guys helped him out of his gloves. Sean spat his mouthguard into his own palm. "I do this for exercise."

"Bullshit," McManus snorted. "You could do that P-90 crap for that. You love this. You crave the sweat and the blood. You're just too much of a pussy to come out from behind that computer screen and train like a real man."

Sean rolled his eyes. "Yes, that's it. You hit it right on the head."

"Come on, O'Malley. Fighting is in your blood. Your dad was going to go all the way."

"Yeah," Sean sighed. "He coulda been a contendah." The reference to Marlon Brando's famous line in *On the Waterfront* was lost on McManus, however.

"Yeah," McManus sighed back. "He just took a bad knock."

The concussion had convinced Sean's dad that boxing wasn't how he wanted to earn a living. But he never lost his love for the sport, going so far as to sign Sean up for the Junior Olympics. But Sean wasn't ever that good. Maybe it was his concentration, like McManus said. His sister could have done it. If his father had ever allowed her to box. Once Mary Katherine set her mind on something, it was as good as done.

And just like that, she was back in his thoughts, haunting him from the grave as sure as she was a *bean sidhe.*

"So tell me about the sweetheart you brought in here." McManus followed him into the locker room and picked up dirty towels, muttering about the pigs who didn't clean up after themselves.

Sean stripped off his clothes and got into the shower before answering.

"She's a girl I'm interested in," he said, finally deciding on the truth. And that was the hell of it. Sean liked everything about her and he wanted to know more.

McManus grunted. "She should have stayed for the fight."

"That would be showing off."

"Nothing wrong with that. It gets the ladies excited to see their men all sweated up after beating up on other guys. What's the word for it? Primal. Yeah."

"Christ, McManus, have you been reading *Cosmo*?" Sean shut off the water and stepped out of the shower, grabbing a towel from the nearby shelf to dry his hair.

"I don't even know what that is," McManus sniffed. "I do know you need a haircut. You look like my sister, Ann."

Sean didn't wince at the word *sister,* but it still hit like a kidney shot.

"Sorry," McManus said when Sean took another towel and wrapped that one around his waist. "If you throw that on the fucking floor, I'll make you eat it." McManus stomped over to the hamper and dumped the armful of towels into it.

Sean was tempted, but didn't feel like antagonizing him today. He finished drying off and balled it up. He shot it over McManus's head for a three-point shot into the hamper.

As Sean was getting dressed, McManus lingered, disinfecting the hot tub and exhaling long suffering sighs. "How's it goin' kid, really? You haven't been yourself."

Waving away McManus's concern, Sean said, "I'm all right." He tucked his shirt into his jeans and buckled his belt.

"Give yourself some time to grieve. Three months isn't a long time."

It could have been yesterday.

"I thought you went a little crazy during the first few weeks."

I did.

"But you're strong, kid," He slapped him on the back. "You snapped back. I'm glad you've got a girl to take your mind off things."

"It's not like that, not yet." Sean finger combed his hair and went to find his jacket.

McManus grunted. "Don't fuck it up. She's a looker." McManus followed him out of the locker room, shutting the lights off behind him.

Oh, he was going to fuck it up all right. The question was if he was going to get hurt in the process, too. He had a feeling it was going to get really complicated, real soon.

Chapter Four

A stripper and a boxer? Sounds fantastic. Get him into bed," Sarah said.

Liz covered the mouthpiece of the phone and checked to make sure Jonathan wasn't in earshot. He was playing in his room and, from the sound of it, too engrossed in his cars to be paying attention to her conversation.

"I'm thinking about it," Liz said in a lowered voice.

"Get out!" Sarah screeched, and Liz had to take the phone away from her ear. "We've got to meet him. Have him come to the FATE meeting on Monday night."

"No. Not yet. I want everyone to meet him outside of FATE first," Liz said.

"Look, if you don't trust him, cut him off. Your instincts are good."

That was the problem; Sean O'Malley made all her senses go so wild, she wasn't sure about anything anymore. She blamed it on lust rearing its ugly head after so many years of abstinence.

"It's not that. I'm just being cautious. For Jonathan's sake, too."

"Well, I guess I can see that," Sarah said. "Take as long as you want on your date, Saturday. I don't mind if Jonathan sleeps over with us." Her husky giggle was full of mischief.

"Not yet," Liz said. "Soon, though. Just not this weekend."

"If you change your mind . . ." Sarah trailed off.

"I'll let you know."

They talked about a few more things before getting off the phone. Christopher had thrown his binkie at Cole when he wouldn't pick him up out of the crib. Then he vaulted out on his own. The two-year-old was running around, causing havoc in his wake. Sarah sounded content—no, better than that, she was happy. Marriage and motherhood definitely agreed with her. Cole smoothed over all her rough spots, polished her up so she shone like the diamond she was. With a wistful smile, Liz slipped the phone into her pocket.

Cinderella.

"Just a fairy tale. A Grimm one." Liz chuckled to herself. It was too bad no one was around to appreciate her humor. Jonathan usually just shook his head and said she was weird. She straightened her suit jacket, wincing at the awkward fit. Even when the seamstress took in darts across the chest, it still didn't hang right. But she couldn't afford a new one and this one was silk and didn't show the use like her other business clothes. With her curly hair in a bun, Liz pulled a few strands down so she didn't look so severe. Easing her feet into a pair of Payless patent leather shoes, Liz figured she looked as academic and professional as she got.

For a moment, she allowed herself to pretend she was back in LA. In 2002, she had offers from every major porn studio. She could choose her leading man, her wardrobe, and even her co-stars. Liz had a platinum American Express with no limit and used it until the mag stripe wore off. She could still remember the account number—not that it worked anymore.

She'd let Steve drive them around in whatever convertible he was borrowing this week. They'd go shopping and buy stuff they didn't need. A Rolex for him. A diamond Movado for her. They'd mug for the cameras. Pose with their fans. Liz remembered this one bikini she wore; it had stars that pasted over her nipples and a sequined skirt. She didn't even bother with underwear. Steve wore a ridiculous banana hammock. They almost got arrested for indecent exposure and lewd acts in public. So they took their lewd acts back to the studio and got paid even more money. Liz stared at her closet, not even one quarter of the size it used to be. Steve's ranch style house in Pasadena had been three times the size of this apartment. And you didn't have to walk up five flights of stairs to get into the place. She could have still been there. Could have still worked for a while longer before the cancer hit.

Liz shook her head clear of the "what if"s. Even if she could go back and do things differently, she wouldn't. Her life with Jonathan was worth more than all the money in the world.

Walking the few steps to her son's room, she leaned against his door frame to watch him play. Someday, they'd move to a bigger place so he wouldn't have to be so cramped. He had his Hot Wheels lined up to drag race across the floor. Snoopy and Sponge Bob were the referees calling the match. He concentrated so fiercely on his toys, she was able to just look at him. He was outgrowing his shirt and the hem on his pants had frayed.

Shit. I just bought those.

For the hundredth time, Liz considered canceling her meeting today. It would take too much time away from him. Time she could spend picking up more design jobs.

No. It's time to start taking my own advice.

"Jonathan, get your shoes on. We're going," Liz called.

He continued to play.

"One," Liz started to count.

"Okay, okay." Jonathan scrambled to his feet and darted past her into the living room to get his sneakers.

She never got to three. Liz often wondered what he thought would happen if she ever did. Would the planet explode? Wouldn't he be disappointed to learn that he'd only lose a few privileges? But for now, the counting kept him on track. He wouldn't ever have to worry about being spanked because she could never raise a hand to him. It would kill her to see him cringing away from her in anticipation of a blow. Liz was a firm believer in talking about things and explaining consequences. Thankfully, she had the patience for it—well, most days, anyway. There were some days when she rolled out the old "because I said so." She remembered cringing from her father's raised hand. He never actually hit her—but she made damn sure she got out of that house and away from his temper the day she turned eighteen.

Jonathan allowed her to hold his hand when they walked down to the subway station, but once they were on the train, he yanked it away.

"I'm a big kid," he told her.

And as much as she was in denial about it, he was getting there. Nine years. Liz held on to the pole as the train hurtled down the tracks. When he was a few months old, she just wanted him to get a little older so she wouldn't have to worry about him being so helpless. Don't wish it away, she had read on the Internet. You'll blink and he'll be all grown up and you'll regret not savoring the moments.

There was no savoring. She had been terrified. Terrified of failing and being homeless. Terrified that SIDS would claim him. Liz didn't sleep peacefully for the first three years of his life. And the next three, she was too busy worrying about putting food on the table than worrying about him growing up and ceasing to be the sweet little toddler who got into everything. But these last three years, if she could have put the brakes on life, she would have. Some days, she wanted a slow motion button so she could watch him explore his world. There were days when she could see her grandfather in him and some days she could see a hint of his father—but that was mostly when he was throwing a tantrum. Steve had been a pouter, too. The last time she heard from that asshole was when she told him she was leaving porn because she was pregnant. He told her to get an abortion and then come out to this rad pool party at some D-list star's house.

She moved to New York instead.

"Why can't I stay home with Mrs. Ritter?" Jonathan whined. "This is boring."

"Life is not always excitement and fun. Get used to it." Liz smiled.

Swinging his legs, Jonathan stuck his lower lip out and grumbled, "Where are we going?"

Butterflies fluttered in her tummy. They were going to chase down a dream. Ever since starting FATE, she had wanted to become a therapist. Graphic design paid the bills, but it didn't make her heart sing. However, to get a license to practice therapy in the state of New York, you needed a Master's degree and a thousand or so hours of monitored counseling.

She never even finished her undergrad degree in English literature at UCLA. There was never any time or need. Now, she wasn't even sure if those old credits would transfer. Becoming a licensed mental health worker just wasn't in the near future—not unless she had some tuition help to get her undergraduate degree in psychology first. Financial aid was one thing, but free tuition was even better. Well, it wasn't really free. She had applied for a scholarship structured like a work study program. It paid in tuition remission instead of a paycheck. She was one of the finalists. If the professor liked her and she got it, Liz would be able to work and take classes while Jonathan was in school. Baby steps. But at least it was forward motion.

"We're going to go see someone who might help Mommy go to school," Liz said.

"Why do you want to go back to school? School is boring." Jonathan looked at her as if she just told him she decided to give up vegetarianism and eat hamburger raw.

"Because it's fun to learn new things." Damn that Common Core curriculum. He'd never had a problem with his attitude about going to school before they rolled it out. "And when you learn new things, you can go on new adventures."

He seemed to consider it. "What kind of adventures? Like Disney World?"

"No, but maybe we can go back again and, this time, take Sarah and Cole and baby Christopher with us."

"Sarah and Cole?" he said, brightening. "Cool. Are they going to give us another vacation?"

"No," Liz said. "And don't you ever ask them to."

"Why not?"

"Because there are a lot of families that they can help who haven't gone to Disney yet. We had our turn."

"It was fun," he said. "My favorite part was the teacup ride."

Liz got so dizzy on that one, the nausea reminded her of the chemo. Shuddering, she said, "I liked the water flume."

"So when can we go back?"

Liz swallowed hard. "When we can afford it."

"I don't see why we can't ask Sarah and Cole. They have lots of money."

He's just a child. He doesn't know what he's saying.

She gripped the pole until she was white knuckled and finally felt she could speak in a calm tone. Shame still poured over her in waves. "Sarah and Cole work very hard for their money."

"Cole doesn't. He 'herited it."

"Cole works very hard." Liz heard the bite in her voice and reined it back when Jonathan's eyes widened. "You earn your own way in this world, baby. Don't expect someone to give you something. If you want it badly enough, you make it your priority and you work hard to get it."

"I'm not a baby," he said, sulkily.

Was that all he heard?

Liz sighed.

"Are you mad at me?"

"No, sweetie, I'm not." Liz was mad at herself. Stupid cancer. All of her savings gone in a year. Stupid expensive surgery. Rotten insurance companies. No. Wrong. Not stupid chemo—that and the radiation were the reasons she was still here, arguing with a nine-year-old about accepting handouts from friends. Blame the cancer, not the cure.

"Can I get a toy today?" Jonathan had moved on while she was fretting about her medical woes.

"No," she said automatically.

"What if I'm good?"

"You're supposed to be good and not get rewarded for it. You don't get a treat for doing what you're supposed to."

"Are we there yet?" He groaned like he was very put out by the situation.

"Is the train still moving?"

Jonathan nodded.

"Then what do you think?" She smiled at him so he knew she wasn't upset.

"How much farther?"

"Two more stops. And if you wait patiently, I'll give you my phone to play with while I'm in my meeting. And then it's pizza time."

"Yes!" He pumped his fist and high-fived her.

And like that, he forgot all about asking Cole and Sarah for money. If only all her problems could be solved by a game of *Angry Birds* and a tomato and basil pie.

They got off the subway and walked the few blocks to the professor's office. They had to pass Washington Square Park where Sean had invited her to go for a picnic on Saturday. Maybe she'd run into him today.

Yeah, right. More than a million and a half people in the city and she was hoping one of them was hanging out by the park, waiting for her to pass by. Still, it was a nice image. Even if the reality was that she would have to introduce him to Jonathan. She might have forgotten to mention her son when they talked.

Liz held Jonathan's hand again as they walked, the promise of her phone keeping him from balking at the contact. She didn't tell Sean about Jonathan because it wasn't any of his damn business. But if Liz was being honest with herself, she didn't tell him about Jonathan because she didn't want to see the interest in his eyes fade just yet. Nothing killed a little flirtation like the introduction of a child. She squeezed Jonathan's hand and blew him a kiss when he looked up.

"Mo-om," he sighed, making the word five syllables long.

"I love you, honey."

"Love you too."

If Sean got group approval, she'd tell him about Jonathan before the first FATE meeting. If he didn't, well, she could just have a quick fling and end things before it got too serious. After all, if her friends didn't like a man she was dating, there was probably something wrong with him. They all hated that asshole Holly had been with before she moved in with Marc.

Checking her phone, Liz confirmed the building number and then walked up the steps. Inside, some students milled in the hallway.

"Excuse me," she asked one. "Can you tell me where Dr. Jenkins's office is?"

"Last door on the left," the student said, pointing.

"Thanks."

The doors were only marked with black numbers. The last door on the left was number seven.

"Lucky number seven," Liz murmured, her thoughts flashing back to a porn set filming a movie of the same name. Seven couples in seven settings having seven orgasms. Not for the first time, Liz was glad that her job now consisted of seven posters, seven websites, and seven business cards. "Let's try for seven classes."

"Are you Professor Donovan?" a pretty young girl asked her.

"No," Liz managed to get out. She plastered on a tight smile and shook her head.

The girl let out a big sigh. "Do you know where I can find her?"

"I'm sorry, I'm new here."

"Okay, thanks." She opened door number five and asked the same question.

For a moment, Liz almost turned and walked out. All the students here were easily ten years younger. She was nearing thirty. When she was their age, she'd just been memorizing her limited dialogue and perfecting her orgasm face while running through most of the positions in the Kama Sutra. Sure, her salary for each film had been nearly as high as what these students paid the school for a semester's tuition, but that didn't matter. What made her think she could do this? Part of her wanted to run out the front door, tugging Jonathan behind her. Liz heard the monkeys in her head strike up the band, playing the same tune they always did. Usually, they waited until the witching hour of three a.m. before starting on her self-esteem.

You're too old.

You're too dumb.

You'll never do this.

You're only good for shaking your boobs at the camera. If you didn't have those, you'd starve.

Okay, the last one was from Steve when she told him she was leaving porn because she was keeping their son. But it was a memorable one. Taking a deep breath, she confronted the monkeys.

Number One: Sean is my age and he's getting his degree.

Just the thought of Sean burned away the monkey's taunts.

Number Two: I am smart and I will do this.

Number Three: I lost my tits to cancer and I'm still here. Nothing is going to stop me.

Liz squeezed Jonathan's hand again and knocked on the door.

"It's open."

Letting herself in, Liz saw a college student texting behind a desk.

"Are you Liz Carter?" he said without looking up.

"Yes." Liz settled Jonathan into the sofa and handed him her phone and a granola bar.

"You can go in." The student indicated an inner door with his head, never missing a beat with his thumbs.

Kissing Jonathan on the forehead, she whispered in his ear, "Be good. If you need me, yell."

"I know," he said exasperated, already lost in the game.

Liz looked at the student behind the desk and back to Jonathan. Maybe they were playing the same game. With a last look at her son, she tapped on the professor's door.

"Come in."

The office looked like it had been ransacked by thieves. Drawers were pulled out and papers flung and stacked everywhere. Liz recognized Professor Jenkins from her picture on the school's website. Jenkins was stabbing keys on an ancient Mac and glaring at the screen.

"Sit down," she said. "Let me save this and I'll be right with you."

Liz removed a stack of papers from a Victorian spoon-back chair that needed reupholstering and eased herself into it, wincing as one of the cushion springs poked her in the ass. She had left the door open so she could keep a casual ear out for Jonathan. While the professor was distracted, Liz risked a glance over her shoulder. He was still engrossed in his game. She willed herself to relax.

"I'm glad you could make it out here today," Dr. Jenkins said, pushing her glasses up to the top of her thin, aquiline nose. For all that her office resembled a disaster area, the professor was elegantly professional. Her chestnut hair was wrapped in a chic bun at the top of her head and she was decked out in a designer suit. The professor wore heavy makeup, but managed to look more like a fashion model than a clown. Liz hoped she looked as good as Jenkins when she was her age. Hell, she'd settle for looking half as put together right now.

"I wouldn't have missed it," Liz said, wringing her hands. "I was very excited to see the scholarship opportunity announced."

"I could tell." Jenkins said. "You were one of our first applicants. Your résumé is impressive." She looked up at her over her glasses. "Nine years of freelancing can take its toll."

Liz nodded. "That's why I'm looking to finish my bachelor's."

"It says here you were an English major at UCLA." Professor Jenkins paused, flipping through her application form.

"I came back to Manhattan when I was pregnant. I grew up in Queens and on the East Coast, and it seemed a better place to raise a child."

That and it removed some of the temptation to star in a fetish film about pregnant women. But Liz didn't think she should share that part with the professor.

"Is that your son out there? He's very well behaved."

"Thank you." Liz concentrated on keeping her breaths even. She hadn't expected to be this nervous.

"Your portfolio is very diverse. I like what you can do. In the event you are selected for the scholarship, I think we can work within the schedule you provided."

"I can start tomorrow."

"Whoa," Professor Jenkins said, holding up her hand. "I like the enthusiasm, but we're still making our final decision. Although, I have to say, you are a strong candidate. If you are chosen, we've got a lot of hoops to jump through and forms to sign. You need to clear everything through the Bursar's office and through Admissions. It's a lot of running around."

"I can do that." Liz was practically bouncing with excitement. Things were finally coming together for her.

"You're going for a bachelor's degree in psychology?" Jenkins looked at the folder to confirm.

"Yes, I am." Tears pricked the corner of her eyes.

"We'll be in touch by the end of the week, hopefully with good news."

"Thank you." Liz rose and shook the professor's hand. She couldn't wait to tell all her friends. Sarah would scream her head off. Sarah suggested going back to college a few years ago, but with the cancer, Liz never saw the point in pursuing her degree.

"What will my duties be?" Liz asked. "If I get the scholarship," she added, even though the vibes she was getting said the scholarship was as good as hers.

"We'll need you to design brochures and posters for the various programs the department will put on. You'll be needed to work at some of the events, but not too often—maybe once a semester."

"As long as I know in advance," Liz assured her. "So I can make arrangements for a sitter for my son."

"Sure, sure. Not a problem." Professor Jenkins stood up and shook her hand. "It'll probably take over a week to get everything in order, but then we can start right in. Thanks again for coming down."

"Oh. No. Thank you. You don't know what this means to me." Liz clasped the professor's hand warmly. "I can't wait to start."

The professor walked her to the door. "Gene, put that damned thing down and do the filing."

The student behind the desk jumped to his feet. "Sorry, Professor."

"Come on, baby," Liz said to Jonathan as she pulled him to his feet.

"I just need to finish this level."

"We're going to have ice cream for dessert." She held out her hand.

"Ice cream?" he said, handing over the phone. "What for?"

"It's time to celebrate!"

Chapter Five

Sean had better ideas for a Saturday morning than wasting it at the clinic waiting for someone he was pretty sure was going to blow him off. But he was just killing time before his date with Liz this afternoon anyway. It was hard to think of anything else. Sean had picked up two large corned beef sandwiches for the picnic, but then he remembered she told him she was vegetarian. He'd stashed those in his fridge for later and begged his party planner neighbor for help.

He was just about to give up when the on-duty nurse let in a nervous looking woman.

"Sabrina?" he asked, rising out of his chair. He wasn't sure if that was her real name. It was the name she used on the DVD she made with Mary Katherine. A quick Internet search gave him her agent's number and he had requested this meeting. It had taken a while, but she called him and made arrangements to come and talk to him.

"Yeah, that's me."

"She said she had an appointment. I can stay if you need me."

"That's all right, Gladys. I'll handle this." The nurse pressed her lips together in a disapproving line and gave him a warning glance over the woman's head. When he went to shake Sabrina's hand, he noticed her pupils were wide and dilated.

Shit. She's high.

Gladys shook her head, but she left the room without a word, shutting the door behind her. Sabrina smiled and sank into the chair opposite his desk, crossing her long pretty legs and showing off her fashionably ripped stockings. She wore a push-up bra, and her ample breasts threatened to spill out of her frilly pink shirt.

Sabrina wasn't his usual client. He saw middle school and pre-teens who needed some help staying out of trouble, with *trouble* broadly defined as anything from acting out in class to using drugs. Sabrina was about his age, but looked a little older. He could see it in the lines by her eyes and mouth, which she tried to hide with heavy makeup.

"Desiree said you were a doctor," Sabrina said, slouching down in the chair and smiling up at him.

It took him a second to connect Mary Katherine's stage name to his sister. "I'm not. Not yet. I'm going for a doctorate."

"She also said you taught at NYU. She was very proud of you." Sabrina gave him a small smile of sympathy.

It hurt.

"I wish she could have told me," he said. "About everything."

Sabrina snorted. "Why are you rooting around in her life? You should just keep the good memories you have of her. She was a really nice girl. And a friend." Sabrina looked down and started chipping the polish off her fingernails.

"I want to understand."

"What's to understand?" Sabrina said. "She wanted to be a dancer on Broadway—"

"A Rockette," he interrupted.

She waved her hand like it didn't matter. "It didn't work out. She tried exotic dancing to pay the rent and then she got into acting."

"How?" Sean already knew the answer to this. Had tracked the guy down, the same way he tracked Sabrina down, but he wanted to hear if her side was different.

"You got a cigarette?" she asked.

"Sorry, don't smoke." Sean pushed a candy dish toward her. "I've got some licorice that might help with the craving."

"Is it Marlboro Light flavored?" Sabrina's laugh brayed out. "What about something else to take the edge off? You can prescribe drugs, right?"

"No." He shook his head.

"How about a drink?"

Sean got up and went over to the small fridge. "I've got water or a soda, which would you like?"

She sighed. "You really are a stick in the mud. I'll take a cola."

Handing her the can, he asked, "Is that what my sister said about me?"

"She said her whole family was like that."

Sean shrugged. "We are who we are."

"Ain't that the truth. My parents are hippies." She gave the peace sign. "I was allowed to smoke pot, have sex, and drink alcohol. I take it Desiree didn't grow up like that?"

Coughing to hide his amusement, Sean said. "No, she had a curfew until she was eighteen. Her boyfriends had to come into the house and talk with my parents before she was allowed to go out. And the only alcohol she ever drank that I knew about was wine during communion."

"So in your message, you said you wanted to know how your sister got into porn? I think it's clear we took different roads to get to the same place."

"Yeah." He sat on the corner of his desk.

Sabrina cracked open the can of soda and took a long gulp. "One of the regulars at the strip joint liked what he saw. So he told a friend of his to check her out. He asked her if she wanted a part in his movie and she said yes."

"Did she know it was pornographic?"

"What would you like to believe?" Sabrina asked. "That she went into it with her eyes open or that they duped her?"

"I want the damn truth."

Sabrina flinched back from him.

"Sorry." Sean moved around and sat down at his desk. Having it between them seemed to make Sabrina more comfortable. She fiddled with something and a quick sideways glance showed him she had palmed a knife.

Way to go, Ace.

He hid his clenched fists in his lap and pasted on a pleasant expression. "Please, just tell me the truth."

Sabrina eyed him. "I don't know what he said to her. I can only tell you how it worked out for me. The first time, he told me that he wanted to film me sucking off some guys. He'd pay me five hundred dollars a dick. I thought he was full of shit, you know?"

Sean nodded.

"But I asked around and it turned out he had a contract for me to sign and everything. He paid right away, too. It was nice not to have to scramble for rent that month."

Did Mary Katherine need the money that badly? She could have come to me for it, if she didn't want to face Dad's "I told you so"s.

"Then the next time," Sabrina said, after another hefty swallow, "he wanted me to fuck them. They were nice guys. He paid me a thousand dollars each. It went from there. Does that shock you?"

When Sean stripped, he made about three hundred to five hundred dollars a night—and that was after tipping out and paying the stage fee. "It's good money."

"Damn good money. Why should I work as a secretary busting my balls for forty hours to earn five hundred dollars a week—if I'm lucky? When I can make four times that amount in one day."

"Six," Sean automatically corrected.

"What?"

"Three guys. Three thousand dollars. Five hundred times six . . . never mind."

Sabrina pointed a finger at him. "Calculator head. Your sister mentioned you had all of Wikipedia up there."

"What else did she say about me?" Sean didn't know why he was torturing himself this way. What did it matter?

"She said you were her baby brother."

"Only by a few years."

"Said you were the golden child."

Sean snorted.

"Perfect in every way."

"She did not," Sean said. Talking to Sabrina reminded him of Mary Katherine. She had been brassy and "in your face," too.

"When she was drunk and maudlin, she did."

Great, I gave my sister an inferiority complex. Was that why she never called me for help?

"How often was that?"

Sabrina played with the hole in her stockings. "Not that often. She was fearless."

She was. That's why her death doesn't make a damn bit of sense.

"I miss her. We used to get dressed up at night and go to the high society bars and have the businessmen buy us dinner and drinks. Then we'd go to the ladies room and sneak out the back door."

"Nice," Sean said, shaking his head. "Those poor guys."

"Those poor guys were thinking they could get free sex for the cost of dinner and drinks. Most of them were married. All of them were rich enough that it never hit their bottom line. We were like Robin Hood."

"Okay, you lost me."

"You know, we robbed from the rich and gave to the poor. Of course, the poor was us."

"Got it."

"So there you have it." She sighed, all the humor fled. Her body looked like a deflated balloon. "I can't believe it. I still think I'm going to see her on the set. Or that she's going to call."

Kübler-Ross's first state of grief: denial

"When did she start taking drugs?" Sean tapped a pencil on his desk, but caught it as the nervous tic it was and set the pencil down.

"I don't know what you're talking about." Sabrina finished the soda and crumpled up the can. She studiously avoided his eyes.

Sean unclenched his jaw and deliberately relaxed his shoulders. He took a deep breath and controlled the tone of his voice with effort. "What made my sister start using?"

"I don't know." She tossed the can in the trash. "Are we done here?"

"What are you on?" Sean asked, leaning back in his chair, attempting to seem non-threatening.

"Fuck you," she said, pushing to her feet.

"I can help you." He launched to his feet, casual pose forgotten.

"I'm not your sister. I don't need saving." She headed for the door.

He followed her. "Why do you take drugs? Is it because of the porn?"

"Why do stockbrokers take drugs?" she countered. "For thousands of different reasons. You'd like to put Desiree in a neat little box and tie her up with a ribbon. Poor little Catholic girl runs afoul in the big city. Drugs led her into porn and killed her. The end. It's not that simple."

Sean's hands fisted. "I know that," he gritted out. "I want to understand."

"Then walk a mile in her stilettos, hot shot. You want to see what happened to her? Live her life. Or do you lack the balls?"

"Been there. Done that. Still don't understand."

"You did a porn? I'm not talking a leaked sex tape with Gladys the disapproving nurse." Sabrina jerked a thumb at the closed door.

Sean repressed a shudder at the mental image. "I stripped for a bit to see if I could figure out why she did it."

Sabrina eyed him up and down. "As what, the nerdy professor?"

"As whatever they told me to be."

"How did it make you feel?"

Sean wasn't used to being on the other end of that question. "Nothing that helped me understand why she overdosed. Look, Sabrina, I'm limited in what I can do. But before you walk out this door, let me try and help. I can recommend a methadone treatment if you're addicted to opioids. Or if you've been using crystal meth like my sister was, we can work out a detox program."

"Addicted?" Her head reared back. "I don't know what you're talking about." She opened the door and strode out.

"Sabrina!" Sean called out. "Please don't go."

But she didn't listen, dodging through the waiting area. Sabrina made a beeline for the front door.

Handled that like a champ.

He rubbed his hand over his face.

✳✳✳ ✳✳✳

Liz was early. Jonathan had been eager to go to Sarah's and Cole's house to swim in their indoor pool. It really was a decadence to float in seventy-degree water in the middle of November in New York City. She was almost sorry she was missing the fun. Baby Christopher looked so cute in his water wings and life jacket, splashing around and chortling.

Sitting on the steps in Washington Park, Liz wrapped her jacket around her and resisted the urge to text Sean. He'd be here in another fifteen minutes—give or take. The weather was mild enough that she was able to enjoy people watching without feeling the cold that much. Liz had dressed casually today, just a pair of soft blue jeans and a Michael Kors red crewneck sweater. She pulled back her shoulder-length hair into a pony tail. Sarah had thrown a Hermes scarf around Liz's neck, claiming the beige and black pattern gave her outfit interest. Liz fiddled with it and hoped she wouldn't lose it.

"Hello, gorgeous," Sean said from behind her.

His low voice sent tingles through her. Yeah, she had it bad. Letting him lift her to her feet, she wondered if he'd kiss her again. But instead of another panty dropping one like last night, he placed a chaste kiss on her cheek.

"You smell nice," Liz said. His cologne had her toes curling and her libido wanted to drag him back to her apartment and have her way with him. But she followed him to the stone chessboard tables set up throughout the park and sat down across from him.

Be good.

He held her hand, stroking his fingers across her knuckles. "Thanks, I took a shower today especially for you," he teased.

"I feel special." She grinned at him.

"Do you play?" Sean held up a bag and shook it.

"Not really."

"I'll show you. If we're eating and not playing, the old guys have a fit."

Liz looked around and saw a few more tables were filling up with young and old, serious players and players who were laughing and chatting more than moving their pieces. Sean handed her the picnic basket and she peeked inside while he set up the board.

There was a crusty loaf of bread, a plastic container of olives, bags of cut up veggies and fruit, and a few other containers that looked like bruschetta, hummus, and dip.

"I should have brought a jug of wine," she murmured, flushing in pleasure that he remembered what she liked. They had chatted about food on Skype; it was the first thing they bonded over. They were both foodies. He told her he thought the copywriter on the Zingerman catalog should win a Pulitzer when she confessed to splurging on wild mugolio pine syrup.

"If you're trying to distract me with love poetry, it's working."

"This is a great spread," she said, laying out the little dip trays. She poured some olive oil from a fancy glass decanter and then ground pepper from a wooden mill on top.

"I cheated," Sean confessed, ripping a piece of bread off the loaf. "My next-door neighbor is a party planner. This is his 'romance basket.'"

"Tell him he gets two thumbs way up." Liz chewed on a jicama stick and looked at the chessboard. She had a vague idea how to play. "I thought there was going to be a concert."

"Yeah, there's a jazz band competition coming up. I figured we should get here early to score some seats."

Dipping the bread into the peppery olive oil, Liz smiled. "This is a pretty good first date." She looked up at him from under her lashes.

He was clean shaven, his strong jaw relaxed into a dreamy grin. His eyes had flecks of green in them, or maybe it was a reflection off his heavy flannel shirt. Liz rubbed her calf over his and watched his eyes widen.

"I want you, too," she told him.

Sean cleared his throat. "Good."

"I'm complicated," she said, stuffing the bread in her mouth before she ruined the moment by saying too much or too little.

"I work with computers a lot. If I can figure out algorithms, I can figure out you." He twisted off the thermos and poured them both a rich, fragrant coffee. "Jamaican Blue Mountain."

"Now, you're just trying to impress me."

"Is it working?" he quirked an eyebrow.

She nodded.

"So what's so complicated?" Sean asked. "You like sex." He ticked off reasons on his fingers. "You want me, too." He waggled his fingers. "But you still don't trust me."

"It's not like that," Liz said. "If I didn't trust you, I wouldn't be here. We're going to meet Sarah and Cole next week, and then the rest of the group."

"I have to get your friends' approval before we can date?"

Liz looked around and lowered her voice. "No, I'm going to fuck your brains out. You're meeting my friends so that they can decide if you're going to be allowed at the FATE meetings."

Sean swallowed. "I can live with that."

"I thought you might."

"So what's so complicated?"

Liz sighed and cupped her hands around the coffee. She drank it black to savor the flavor of the expensive blend, but he—or his neighbor—had thought to pack almond milk in case she wanted to lighten the coffee. "I almost want to fuck you first and then tell you in case you go screaming off into the sunset."

"I solemnly swear to fuck you first before running away in terror." Sean held up a hand.

Liz laughed.

"Are you going to tell me or should I guess?"

"I'm getting to it," she said, looking away at the band setting up their instruments.

"Did you, y'know, catch something?" he asked softly.

"What?" she screeched. "No. Cancer." At his expression, Liz elaborated. "Sorry, you threw me for a moment. I've tested negative for all STDs. You?" She arched an eyebrow at him.

He nodded. "Clean."

That was a relief. "I'm on the pill, too."

"Good," he flashed a wolf's smile at her before getting serious. "Now, what's this about cancer?"

Liz blew out a sigh. "It's in remission. I had a rough couple of years. I had radiation and chemo, and . . . surgery." She forced herself to look at him. "You said you saw my movies, right?"

"Yeah . . ." He tilted his head as though he was trying to figure out where she was going with this.

"Notice anything different?"

When he continued to look at her, she thrust her chest at him.

"I-I thought you were just wearing a tight bra," he stammered.

"Sean, there's not a bra in the world that can make double Ds look like Bs. And if there is, I wouldn't want to wear it. I had to have a double mastectomy." Her voice hitched on the last word.

"I'm so sorry," he said. "That sounds traumatic."

"It was better than dying." Liz gave a short laugh. "But it's been a transition." She took a deep breath. "I got the reconstruction surgery, but there's no sensation in them. They're just bumps that make my sweaters hang right." Liz waved her hands over her chest. "So that's kind of a bummer. Is it a deal breaker?" She risked a look at him.

"Not even remotely," he said, his voice husky.

I will not cry. He says that now, but wait until he sees the scars. Wouldn't he be constantly comparing my new body to my old voluptuous one?

"Disappointed?" She kept the tremor out of her voice with iron will.

"Just means I can spend more time playing with your pussy." He shot a look of pure sin at her that left her gaping.

Liz swallowed hard. "There is that."

"So any more complications I should be aware of?"

Jonathan. No, my son is not a complication.

Yet, she didn't bring him up. "It's . . . uh, been a while for me." She cleared her throat. "Years—even before the cancer." Liz could only look at him for short moments at a time because she was afraid he'd see the need in her eyes. The dusting of scruff on his jaw tempted her to kiss his soft lips.

"Why?" He frowned at her. "Does it have something to do with why you left the industry?"

"You could say that," Liz hedged, risking another glance at his intense, dark eyes. She could get lost in them.

"Were you . . . raped?" he asked gently.

"Jesus Christ, you jump to conclusions," she said, smacking her hand on the table. He was easier to fantasize about when he wasn't talking shit.

"Well, I don't know. You're being so mysterious, I'm thinking worst-case scenario." He threw up his hands in aggravation.

"No, it was nothing like that. I just outgrew the porn industry. It got boring." That wasn't a total lie. It had started getting old. All the excitement was taken out of sex. It was a job and it had gotten harder and harder to have a real orgasm as time went on. "Sex wasn't a priority. I didn't have anyone I wanted to be intimate with." Liz looked around to see if anyone was listening in on the conversation. "Until now."

"Okay, so we can take it slow. I've got some issues, too." He was about to say something when the first band started warming up. "So much for our chess game," Sean said, gesturing to the board.

"Lunch was fantastic." She helped him pack up the leftovers.

They cleaned up the table and vacated it for two intense looking gentlemen wrapped in wool trench coats. Liz saw them setting up a timer and putting out gorgeous, hand-carved chess pieces. The band opened up with swing music and she and Sean danced. Gasping for breath and giggling, Liz was relieved when the second band played slower, a soulful jazz that eased over the park like a cozy blanket.

Sean wrapped his arms around her while they watched the musicians. Liz felt his hardness through the thick fabric of her jeans. He rocked his body in time with the bass line and she wanted to rub her backside against the length of him. Sean slipped his hand under her sweater, his fingers tracing over her stomach. She tensed, wondering if he'd forget and go higher to cup a breast that was no longer normal. But he didn't and she relaxed against him as he continued to caress her rib cage and side.

She wanted his fingers lower, but the crowd was packed tightly around them now. They would surely notice if she unzipped her pants. Tilting her head to the side, Liz willed him to nuzzle her neck. Pulling off Sarah's five hundred dollar scarf, she stuffed it in her coat pocket. Sean didn't disappoint, pressing soft, wet kisses at the juncture of her throat. When he started to use his teeth, Liz couldn't help the little sigh that escaped her.

"Like that?" he said in her ear. His hot breath sent shivers over her sensitized body.

"You want to get out of here?" she answered.

"I thought you'd never ask."

"Let's go to your place," Liz said. Jonathan's toys were all over the apartment and she didn't want to have that conversation yet. Not when she was so wet and shaking—she was about to slam Sean against a statue and have her way with him.

"My place?" He coughed. "Uh, my roommates are studying for a big exam."

"Fuck," she said, her desire tempered by frustration.

"I know a place. Not far from here."

"Hurry," she whimpered.

Chapter Six

Liz recognized the building Sean was steering her toward with a slow dread. The quick walk didn't do anything to calm her raging hormones, but the sight of where they were going had her putting on the brakes. It was an NYU building, the same building where Professor Jenkins had her office.

"I can't go in there," she said.

"Huh? Why? There's no one around. It's a Saturday. The last place anyone wants to be is their advisor's office on a weekend."

Liz let him pull her inside. He was right. There wasn't anyone milling about the corridors. But if they got caught, she would lose that scholarship for sure. "What if someone catches us?"

"We're not trespassing. I'm . . . I'm a student here. And besides, we'll have our clothes on."

"We will?" she said mournfully, before remembering that she didn't want to be caught naked and doing the wild thing in the place she was going to work.

"Slow. This is going to happen slow." He kissed the tip of her nose. "I'm still going to make you come, however."

Liz was speechless as he propelled her down the halls. Thankfully, they didn't go into number seven. Liz didn't think she could handle that, working in the same office they fooled around in. She'd never get anything done.

Sean pulled her into office number three and locked the door behind them.

"How did you know this place would be empty?" Liz said.

"I didn't."

Not bothering with the lights, he pulled her into her arms. Oh, that kiss. The same fierce one he plastered on her the other night. Thoughts fled as her hands greedily clutched his shoulders. Liz was dimly aware he was backing her up. When her knees hit something, a couch maybe, they sank down on it.

Liz let him roll them so they were on their sides. Her mouth never left his and it was luxurious to just kiss. No one ever wanted to see kisses on camera. It was boring. In porn, mouths were for moaning or full of cock or pussy. This sweet glide, the desperate press of lips, made Liz ache. Sean popped open the button of her jeans and tugged them halfway down her hips. She unbuttoned his flannel shirt and splayed her hands over his t-shirt, which covered the hard muscles on his chest. He was so warm and the rich scents of musk, soap, and masculinity had her eyes rolling back in her head.

"You are so gorgeous," he muttered.

"I want to touch you." Liz tugged his T-shirt out of his pants. Gliding her hands over his chiseled abs, she sighed. "It's been so long."

Sean eased her jeans down past her knees. As he ravaged her neck with quick nips and the rough abrade of his five o'clock shadow, Liz opened her legs to give him better access. "Yes," she moaned when he pushed aside the damp silk of her panties.

"So wet and creamy." Sean took her mouth again, his tongue exploring hers. Meanwhile, his fingers were demanding on her clit.

Digging her fingers into his shoulders, Liz met his kiss with an intensity that pressed him back against the couch.

Voices in the hallway and the sound of a light turning on made them freeze.

"Shh," he said, unnecessarily, in her ear, his fingers still flickering fast and slick over her throbbing bud.

Laughter echoed down the hall and another door closed.

"Are we okay?" Liz murmured, almost afraid to breathe. Her body was twitching with each stroke.

"Maybe." He kissed the corner of her mouth and held her tightly. But the waiting was taking too long, so she trailed her tongue over his lips until he was kissing her breathless again.

So good. So damned good.

Her legs shook and the sweet release took her by surprise. Liz gasped, a high shriek into his mouth as her orgasm shuddered through her. She felt light, free, endorphins wildly spinning her.

Sean lifted his head up and then grinned at her. "Shh."

"You shush," she stage whispered, hitting him in the chest because his fingers were still dancing inside her and her legs were spasming in pleasure.

He eased up his stroke, murmuring against her mouth, "I wanted to do that since the first time I saw you on Skype."

He pulled his fingers out and licked them. She grabbed his hand and deep throated his fingers. Sean grunted at the suction.

Tossing her hair back, Liz slid off the couch and on her knees. "Know what I've been wanting to do to you?" Her hands went to the button on his jeans.

"You don't have to," he panted.

Liz rubbed her palm over the hard bulge in his pants. "This is telling me otherwise." Rubbing her cheek over the length of him, she turned her head and blew. Her hot breath warmed the material over his cock.

Sean leaned into the caress, his mouth open in a moan of pleasure. Taking that as a request, Liz unzipped his jeans and folded down his boxers until his cock sprang out. Liz clutched the hard shaft, fondling it over her face and neck. For a moment, she almost put it between her breasts—old habits die hard. To cover her mistake, she took his cock as far down her throat as she could.

She heard his head hit the wall.

"Sweet lord," he drawled, the Irish coming out. It turned her on, and she wanted him to say something else in that sexy accent. Slowly working her way up, she gripped his long shaft until all that was in her mouth was the head of his cock. Smearing the salty precum over her lips, Liz looked up at him. His fingers were clenched in the couch. Sean's heavy breaths echoed in the room. His eyes were squeezed shut.

"Talk to me. It gets me off to hear your brogue."

"Oh darlin'," he grinned.

She shivered and swirled her tongue over the head of his cock.

"I canna wait to fuck you."

Liz licked him faster.

"I'm going to have you on yer hands and knees," Sean drawled. "With yer sweet ass in my hands. I'm going to pound that pussy until you scream my name."

Taking him down her throat again, Liz sucked. His sexy voice made her so ready for him to do what he was promising.

"And then," he growled, his hand suddenly in her hair. He pushed her deeper. "Then I'm going after your sweet ass."

Liz moaned. She liked his dirty talk and the way he was shoving her head up and down on his cock. It was like he was fucking her face, nice and slow. She could picture what his cock would be like inside her. Want and need exploded in her and she sucked him harder, faster, desperate to feel him spill down her throat.

Footsteps again. Liz froze. Sean held her head on his cock. The knob to the office jiggled. Liz raised wide eyes at Sean. He was looking at the door.

"Where are my damned keys?" a man's voice from outside said.

Sean pulled on Liz's hair, but instead of having her stop, he was encouraging her to continue. They were going to get caught. Unless, she could make him come before whoever was out there found his keys.

Doubling her efforts, Liz went all out, trying to keep the sucking sounds to a minimum.

"Dear God," Sean gasped.

With one last rattle on the door and an irritated sigh, the footsteps moved away. The hall light went out. They heard the front door close. Liz lavished her tongue around his shaft and head.

His fingers untangled from her hair. "I'm going to come."

Liz didn't relent, taking him deep into her throat, until he cried out, arching into her mouth.

She swallowed his hot bursts of pleasure and climbed back on the couch with him. Holding him in her hand still, Liz leaned in for another kiss. Sticky and hot, he was still hard as she stroked him.

"Are you trying to kill me?" he asked, the Irish still apparent in his voice. He cupped her face and kissed her nose, cheeks, and mouth.

"That was an adventure," Liz panted. She was on edge, wanting to shuck her pants completely off and impale herself on him. "More."

"My pleasure," he purred, laying her flat on the couch.

She kicked off her shoes as he shimmied her pants off. "Take me. Fuck me hard."

"Mmm." He spread her legs, brushing his hands over her soft curls. "That's not taking things slow."

"I don't want slow, damn it. I want you inside of me."

Sean moved between her legs, but it was his tongue that entered her. Liz clamped her hands on his head, guiding him.

"I want, I want," she gasped out, unable to ask him again. He spread her wide open and was enjoying teasing her, dipping his fingers in and out of her. When he began to probe her ass, she whimpered. She'd take anything right now. His tongue was lapping over her hard, pulsating bud. Two fingers stroked in and out of her pussy, while his pinky toyed at the other opening.

"Sean," Liz cried, her head whipping back and forth. "Fuck me. Please fuck me."

"Not on a dusty old couch," he said. "When I fuck you, it'll be in a bed and I'm going to come in every hole you have."

It was the Irish. It was the dirty talk. Hell, it was his fingers and that talented tongue when it went back to her clit. Liz dissolved into a moaning, panting, mess of emotions. "Please," she whispered. "Please." The room was spinning.

God, that was incredible.

Sean kissed her as he pulled her pants back up and buttoned them. Liz trailed her fingers through his hair. Flipping her shirt up, he kissed her belly button. She shrieked and pushed the shirt down. Nope. Not ready for him to see her breasts, or lack thereof. There was too much light in the room. Maybe if it was pitch dark. That she was even considering taking off her sweater was almost as mind-blowing as her orgasms had been.

"Not yet," she said, and to make it up to him, reached for his cock to guide it inside her.

"Behave," he said, sitting next to her and fixing his clothes.

"I wasn't done with that," she pouted.

He cuddled her on his lap. "It's enough for one day, sweetheart. Can't catch up on what you were missing all at once."

Liz nibbled on his ear. "I'd like to try."

She sighed as he rubbed circles over her back. His shoulder was a nice place to lay her head. "So where does the brogue come from? I only hear it when you're hot and bothered by something."

"My parents are from Ireland. They moved to Long Island shortly after my sister was born."

Liz felt him tense, the carefree lover fading away. She lifted her head to look at him. "What's wrong?"

He sighed and shook his head. "Nothing."

"Are you close with them?"

"Not really. Da is . . . let's say, set in his ways and my Mum could give Ghandi a run for his money in the martyr category. They're good people. Strong Roman Catholic beliefs. We're just not close."

Liz tried to hear what he wasn't saying in the silence that followed.

"And your sister?" she prompted when it seemed like he wasn't going to continue.

He flinched. "She's dead."

"Oh, I'm so sorry."

"Three months ago."

"Sean," she pulled herself up to look at him. "That's right around the time we started talking. You never said anything."

"It had just happened. It was too raw. It's still too raw."

Liz couldn't breathe as shame flooded her. Sean had reached out for FATE and she had denied him that comfort. "I'm so sorry. I didn't know."

"I didn't want you to know."

"How did she die?"

Liz didn't think he was going to answer her. He kept rubbing her back in a slow, soothing rhythm as though she was the one who needed comfort, not him. She clutched him tighter, making sure he knew she was there for him.

"Overdose." He finally clipped out.

"That's horrible." Liz leaned her head back on his shoulder and just held him.

Another empty silence fell and she could practically hear him thinking.

"Did you ever do drugs?" he asked.

"Not even a joint," Liz said.

"Why not? I thought all porn stars got high."

Something in his voice made her shift around so she could look him in the eyes. She thought she heard accusation, but there was only sadness on his face. "There were a lot of temptations in LA. Drugs were plentiful in the industry, even if the directors played lip service to them being forbidden. There were performance enhancing drugs on set. Off the set, there was enough weed to get a small village in Thailand high. Coke, oxy, meth . . ." she trailed off when Sean tensed again. "So it was available, but no one forced it on you. Why do you ask?"

Another silence. Liz was watching him this time. His face was expressionless and his eyes were far away. When he came back to her, he seemed exhausted. As if his journey had been a physical one.

"No reason," he said, clearing his throat.

✳✳✳ ✳✳✳

Sean didn't blame Liz for being confused. His mind was scattered into a million pieces. So much for having a casual fling while he found out what demons forced Mary Katherine to start taking meth. Liz was amazing, making him lose sight of reality. He wanted to be the ex-stripper boxer/student she thought he was. What would she do when she realized he nearly fucked her in the TAs' shared office? He looked over at the mountain of paperwork in his inbox. He had only himself to blame for assigning research papers so soon after midterms.

He was so freaking stupid. Liz was going to hate him. And he didn't blame her. Right now, he hated himself.

Why couldn't he just come clean and tell her the truth?

Because she felt too damn good in his arms. He should have never touched her, never tasted her. He could have remained an observer and guarded his heart if he kept everything platonic. Of course, his ethics were shot in this area anyway. He didn't have informed consent. But he didn't think he'd get real information if Liz or her friends knew he was looking for correlations between porn stars and drugs. He tried other sources and was only told what they thought he wanted to hear. Liz was different. She was genuine. Too bad he couldn't be. He kissed her forehead.

"We should leave before someone comes looking to see who was doing all that screaming," he said, letting his arms drop.

"It wasn't just me, buster."

"Come on, let's walk around and I'll grab you a cab." He lifted her off him and pulled them both to their feet.

"Yeah, it is getting late. Can you come to dinner next Saturday at my friends' house?"

"Sure, we'll Skype during the week if you want," he said. And then because he wanted more of her, "Unless you want to see me sooner?"

Glutton for punishment.

Her breath quickened, and he hauled her to his side in a tight embrace. "I'd like that, but my weekdays are so hectic."

He nodded. He was a little overbooked with everything, too. He had cases to review and McManus was trying to get him to spar with Donovan. Not to mention the Introduction to Social Work class was going to be starting in a few weeks. All he wanted to do, though, was roll around naked on the sheets with Liz. But first, he'd have to explain why his apartment didn't look like your typical undergrad's.

More lies.

His head ached. They walked for a few blocks arm in arm before Sean saw a taxi he could flag down. The driver pulled up to the sidewalk.

"How about a dirty Skype session?"

Sean fumbled in the act of opening the car door for her. "What?"

"Wednesday night. Eleven p.m. I'll put on a show for you. Then next week, it'll be your turn."

"A show?" he said.

"I'll masturbate for you. Or maybe, I'll fuck myself with a dildo? I'll surprise you. Don't worry. I can be very creative." She opened the door and blew him a kiss.

He was still staring dumbfounded at the cab when it pulled away.

Chapter Seven

So your turn, Liz," Sarah turned to her with an evil grin. "What's new with you and our prospective member Sean?"

Instinctively, Liz looked to make sure Jonathan's door was still closed. Monday nights were always rough now that his bed time was later. She'd moved the FATE meetings from 8:00 p.m. to 10:00 p.m. to give her more time with him. They had a nice supper together and read a few more chapters of Harry Potter. He was supposed to be sleeping soundly, but lately he had been sneaking out of his room and listening to the grownups.

"Why are you keeping this Sean all to yourself?" Honey said. The delicate brunette balanced a teacup and plate of crudités on her lap. She was bundled up in wool leggings and a belted tunic that made her look sophisticated and trendy. Liz would have looked like an Eskimo.

"It could be because he's a hot stripper who boxes." Sarah was far too gleeful than the situation merited. A stunning blonde, she oozed sexuality with each swing of her long legs. Eschewing the tea and going straight for the wine now that she was no longer breast feeding, Sarah looked like all she needed was a bowl of popcorn to enjoy the show.

Liz stuck her tongue out at her. "Ex-stripper. And he's enrolled in college courses to get a degree. Which reminds me—"

"What does he box? Candy?" Peter hitched his hip on her TV armoire and did his best to look crisp and dapper.

Liz felt positively frumpy next to her glamorous friends. "He teaches boxing to at-risk youths at a gym in Queens. He took me on a tour of the place; it's really nice."

Peter and Sarah exchanged exaggerated winks. "How was the locker room?"

"Guys," Brian admonished. He had just come from the garage and was dressed in jeans and a T-shirt that was spattered with dirt and grease. He sat on the floor because he hadn't wanted to get her couches all dirty. Not that she cared. They were curb finds and, while she was grateful to have them, they weren't the kind of furniture you enveloped in plastic.

Everyone looked at Brian. He seemed uncomfortable with the attention. "Liz?"

"Thank you, Brian. What I was trying to say is I made a big step last week. You all know that I've wanted to go back and get my degree, but what you might not know is that I'm not going to be an English lit major."

"Not a lot of jobs advertising for that, is there?" Peter said with a toast of his tea.

"I got the call today. I applied for a working scholarship and got it. So I'm going back to school to get a psychology degree." Liz looked around at her friends' faces and saw happy surprise. "I want to be a therapist."

"That's the perfect thing for you," Honey said, setting her plate and tea down to clap her hands excitedly.

Sarah made a "squee" sound and tackled her on the couch for hugs. Peter leaned in and kissed her cheek once the wrestling match was done.

"It's about time," he said. "You're going to be great."

"Cool." Brian gave her a thumbs up.

"Just let us know if you need someone to watch Jonathan." Sarah resumed her seat and poured both of them more wine.

"I've got it all arranged. My classes and the work for the scholarship will happen while he's at school. So I'll still be around to walk him home and spend some time with him before homework and bed. Of course, I might have to have one of you pick him up from school from time to time. Is that okay?"

"Of course it's okay," Sarah said, looking around the group and getting nods in return. "I'll go with you a few times this week so the school gets to recognize I'm your friend. That way if you ever need me to pick up Jonathan, they'll see a familiar face."

"Great. I'll put all of you on the pick up/drop off list." Liz grinned. "Like I said, it won't happen a lot. Thanks, guys. I really appreciate it."

"You're going to do all this and your graphic design business?" Peter raised an eyebrow. "We're going to have to get you a red cape."

"I found out about the scholarship through my cancer support group." Liz said. "I can take classes for free as long as I put in a certain amount of hours. There is one thing, though." It was what was messing with her sleep at night.

"What?" Brian asked, looking ready to go to battle for her.

She gave him a grateful smile. "There's this stupid morality clause in it. If I'm caught doing anything that embarrasses the school, I'm out. And I'll have to pay back the school for the classes I took."

"That's bullshit. That can't even be legal," Sarah said.

"Well, you're not going to do anything like that so you have nothing to worry about," Honey reassured her.

"Unless someone recognizes me." Liz shrugged. "Although, with these chopped off, it's not likely." She gestured to her chest.

"Then stop worrying about it." Peter joined her on the couch and put a comforting hand on her knee. "It's been nine years. That's a lifetime in porn. The young stars don't even know who you are. And the people who watched you have moved on to those new young things."

"Thanks a lot," Liz groaned. "I feel as sexy as a truck most days anyway."

"Which brings us back to the ex-stripper," Sarah said. "Why isn't he here tonight?"

"Because I'm a terrible person." Liz put her hands over her face.

"Yes, I say that all the time." Peter rolled his eyes.

"What heinous crime did you commit now?" Honey poured herself another cup of tea and started to nibble on a shortbread cookie.

"Sean and I started emailing and texting about three months ago. We hit it off. I liked him, and I thought the group might be good for him." Liz started to stack empty dishes. Sarah took them from her and brought them into the kitchen.

"I'm listening," she called back.

"I decided to Skype with him a few times before inviting him to a FATE meeting. We talked and texted for weeks. He's really funny. He'll see a typo on a sign or a crazy poster and send it to me. I like him. And yet, there was something off. He had secrets."

"Sweetie, we all have secrets," Honey said.

"I know, but something didn't feel right. However, his references all checked out, so I decided to meet with him. And he's a great guy, so big and protective, and at the same time, sweet and nice."

"You're right." Peter gripped her knee and shook it. "Mr. Perfect is hiding something. Trust your instincts."

"Peter," Sarah scolded. "So, I still don't get what you did that was so terrible. You were trying to protect us."

"I guess I'm a little gun-shy after that tabloid reporter tried to fake his way in." Liz sighed. What a scumbag that piece of shit had been. A quick Google search and she knew his real name-and all the rags he was stringing for. He published half-truths and mean-spirited articles. She called him out on his bullshit story and he didn't even have the grace to be embarrassed. "But Sean's not like that. In fact, he and I were talking last Saturday and he told me his sister died. It was the reason he reached out to us. I feel so bad. We could have helped, supported him during a horrible time, but I was too afraid to let him in."

"No," Honey said. "You did the right thing. You couldn't know he was grieving."

"Grief is a funny thing," Sarah added.

"So make it up to him. Tell him to come next Monday." Peter snitched a marzipan cookie off the tray, just as Brian reached for it. Brian settled for one with a cherry on top.

"Really?" Liz sniffed. "You sure?"

"I'll tell you what. I'll give them the complete rundown after our dinner Saturday. Cole and I get to meet Mr. Perfect." Sarah was practically wriggling with excitement.

"Well, that's no fair," Peter said. "What restaurant? Pol and I will just happen to be there too."

"Oh, hell no." Liz shook her head.

"Mrs. Ritter is going to watch Jonathan? Or would you like Marc and me to babysit?" Honey cut into the conversation, frowning at Peter, who let her disapproval roll off his nicely tailored jacket's shoulders.

"Mrs. Ritter said she'd do it. It's not going to be a late night," Liz assured her.

"Well, at least the dinner won't run late. Is Mr. Perfect going to stay over?" Sarah asked.

"You have to stop calling him that. What if you slip up? Geez. I'm not sure. I still haven't told him that I'm a mother."

Liz hadn't expected the silence that fell with that statement.

"What? I didn't think it mattered at first. Then there wasn't a good place to throw it in conversation. 'Oh, by the way, I have a nine-year-old son. I hope you like Minecraft and Star Wars because that's all he talks about.' Once I got really interested in Sean, I didn't want to lose him when he found out I was a package deal."

"If he lets that get in the way of a relationship, you'd be better off without him." Honey crossed her arms.

"I know that, but he's the first man I've been attracted to in . . . well, forever. So I figured I'd have my way with him and if he turned out to be an asshole, well at least I got laid. Right?"

Sarah high-fived her. "Flawlessly logical. I'm in awe."

"So, this is serious?" Honey asked.

"I'll let you know by the weekend. I'm going to tell him on Wednesday. If he runs for the hills, maybe I'll be solo on Saturday," she said to Sarah. "Unless Jonathan wants to be my date. I think he'll still fit in the suit he wore to Honey's wedding, if I let the hems out." Liz blew out a sigh. "He's getting so big. Anyway," Liz dusted off her hands. "Enough about me. It's Brian's turn. Do you have anything you'd like to share?"

"I'm seeing someone," he admitted.

"O-M-G, it's like Cupid is on the rampage," Peter said. "Who's the lucky girl?"

"She's in the industry still." He shrugged. "Mostly, she does gay for pay and I'm all right with that."

"What's her name?" Liz asked.

"Sabrina. She's hot."

"Of course she is." Sarah grinned. "Which studio is she working with? I didn't think there were any left in New York."

"Chalice Films, mostly. Some indies. I think she even worked for Luscious Studios for a time. You're right, there aren't a lot of places around here, what with all the hoops and mazes Giuliani set up. LA is still the porn capital of the world."

Liz thought that was the most she's ever heard Brian say in one go.

"Have you thought about getting back into the business so you could be her cameraman?" Peter asked.

"Sure, but not seriously. I'd either become a jealous asshole or I'd stop caring. I'll stick with the cars." He shrugged. "Tempting, though. Sometimes I think going back into porn would be like selling my soul. Sure, I can do it. The money is prime. The eye candy amazing. But it would change me. I'd become more jaded, cynical. Restoring a GTO doesn't make me feel empty inside. Just the opposite." Brian looked at the beer in his hand. "Maybe I should've had dinner before drinking these. I'm starting to ramble."

"It's okay." Liz had been afraid to breathe during his speech. That he trusted them to open up this much after all this time was amazing. She had to blink back tears.

"I hear what you're saying." Sarah nodded.

"Yeah, you nailed it." Peter went over and clapped a hand on Brian's shoulder.

"You do have a point about the soul selling. You think you'd get used to it. Become jaded, like you say. It can be wearying." Holly looked down into her teacup, as though she was trying to read her fortune in the tea leaves.

"Thanks." Brian got up and collected his empties, putting them in the recycling bin. "I'm actually going to go. Otherwise I'll start getting sentimental and shit."

"Brian," Liz said. "Do you think Sabrina would want to come to a FATE meeting?"

"She's not giving up the life yet. She still likes it."

"I was still in," Honey pointed out. "Granted, I was completely lying to you all about that. But I loved being in this group. It got me through some tough times."

He shrugged. "I'll ask. Thanks."

"Let me know." Liz handed him his coat. "Shoot me a text when you get home."

"Yes, Mom." Brian leaned in and kissed her cheek.

✳✳✳ ✳✳✳

Liz couldn't concentrate at all on Wednesday. They barely got through Jonathan's homework without tears—on both their parts. Then, they finished the Harry Potter book and didn't have the next one. So that caused a minor meltdown that ended as soon as she downloaded book two on her phone. Should she have capitulated? No. Did she need to in order to avoid throwing a tantrum herself? Yes.

She hit the wine after tucking him in and would have happily finished the bottle if it wasn't for her Skype date with Sean. They had only texted a few times during the week because both of them were crazy busy.

After making sure Jonathan was sound asleep, Liz locked her bedroom door. She was more nervous now than she'd been at her first porn shoot. At least then she could hide behind her double Ds. All she had now was an electric blue vibrator and a leather vest. Checking herself in the mirror, Liz adjusted the black leather stretched across her chest and made sure it showed just a V of cleavage and nothing else. The sparkly Swarovski crystal in her belly button should draw his eyes away if anything did shift.

Maybe she should go for the nipple tattooing. She'd at least look more natural.

Baby steps.

Liz fixed her makeup, painting on another coat of lipstick so her mouth was plump and red. She put on her false eyelashes and darkened up the kohl around her eyes. The Skype camera tended to wash out colors, and she wanted to be as vivid to Sean as possible. Styling her hair so it was wavy and wild, Liz was glad it had finally grown out. When she lost most of her hair after the chemo, she'd looked weird, as she couldn't bring herself to shave her head completely. Instead, she wore pretty scarves and tried to pretend she was still normal. When her hair started to grow back, Liz burned every one of those damned scarves so she'd never have to see them again. Now, she wished she had a couple she could use as props. They could be blindfolds. Or restraints.

Liz had been going back and forth about how she was going to present herself all week. She tried the laptop in several positions before the camera was aimed just right. Darting a glance at the clock, Liz realized she had ten minutes to get it together and finalize the details.

She slipped on a black thong and laced up her thigh-high boots. Skype dinged.

It was now or never.

Pulling on a kimono robe, she answered the call.

❋❋❋ ❋❋❋

Sean had convinced himself she had been kidding, teasing him so he would fantasize about her all week. Never in a million years did he think she'd answer looking like that.

"Wow," he breathed. "Hey, sexy. I wish I was there."

Liz tilted her head to the side. "I've got a confession to make," she said.

"Have you been a bad girl?" Sean was getting into this. He wanted to take off his clothes and stroke himself. She made every little annoyance and frustration he had dealt with this week fade into the background.

"I haven't been completely honest with you."

Sean's gut clenched. Was this about the industry? Was she finally going to tell him something that would unlock Mary Katherine's death? His hard-on fled as fast as it came.

"Tell me," he said, noting she bit her lip and was blinking fast.

"I just want you to know, that if you decide to dump me or make some lame excuse not to see me again, you're going to miss the greatest show of your life." She stuck out her tongue at him.

It broke the tension and they both laughed. "Just tell me, you goof."

"I have a son."

Sean felt like he got some chin music. He rubbed the nape of his neck, sure his head rocked back from the impact of that blunt statement. "You do?"

"Yes," Liz rushed through the rest. "He's in third grade. His name is Jonathan and he likes pizza, ice cream, and Transformers."

"Well, who doesn't really?"

"Transformers are not the things on top of telephone wires; they're toys that change from robots to cars."

"I'm aware. I used to be a little boy." He might even still have his old Bumblebee. It changed from a car, to a plane, to a . . .

"He's a sweetheart," Liz said. "And I didn't tell you about him because I was a coward. I didn't want to scare you off."

"Why would I be afraid of an elementary school kid? Does he bite?"

"No, he doesn't bite." Liz shook her head and grinned.

"Do I get to meet him?" Sean asked, the knot in his chest unraveling when he realized that this was her big news.

Liz narrowed her eyes at him. "You want to meet him?"

"Sure," he shrugged. "We can go out for pizza. Or we can go to the gym. Anything you want. I'll let you decide."

"Well, this was a heck of a lot easier than I thought." Liz deflated. "This is the whole reason why I didn't bring you home last week. I didn't want you to step on a Lego and I'd have to explain."

"I like Legos," he said. "I used to build spaceships with them."

Liz nodded. "Cars. It's all about cars for Jonathan."

"You don't have to hide anything from me."

He felt like such a hypocrite. Now would be the perfect time to tell her about Mary Katherine. But what if she turned off the webcam and stopped answering her phone when she learned he'd been lying? He'd miss out on meeting Jonathan, who was clearly a kid with good taste. And he'd miss out on seeing Liz, naked or fully clothed. He wanted to keep seeing her.

"Forgive me for keeping my son a secret?" Liz asked.

Sean nodded. "Sometimes people tell lies because they're afraid the truth will destroy something really amazing."

"Exactly," she said.

"Of course I forgive you. Because there's nothing to forgive." Sean hoped that one day she'd say the same thing to him.

"Well then," Liz said. "I believe I promised you a good time." She slowly untied the knot holding the kimono closed. Shrugging one creamy shoulder out and then the other, Liz let him look at her leather vest for a moment. He was more interested in seeing underneath it, but he didn't want to get greedy. She shook her hair so her black curls bounced around her shoulders.

"Gorgeous," he breathed. "I want to lick every inch of you."

Liz let the rest of the kimono fall away. She was wearing a teeny black confection over her pink mound. His eyes captured every move her fingers made as they slid down over her chest to her belly button ring. She toyed with it before stretching the string of her black panties, tempting him.

"Like what you see?"

"Yeah," he said, his voice hoarse. He cleared it. "I want to play with your pussy again. I liked how you squirmed and came all over my fingers."

Her thighs quivered. Sean wanted to bite them.

"I've been thinking about last Saturday all week," Liz said, reaching for the blue vibrator. Turning it on, she ran it up and down her legs, easing them apart until they were spread wide for the camera. Sean could see that she was wet and ready. He let out a groan.

Liz slowly closed her legs, but before disappointment hit, she slid the thong down her toned legs until it disappeared off screen.

"Me too." Sean's mouth hung open as she pushed the electric blue toy into her wet slit.

"You're not just saying that because you want to watch me stick this—" She rubbed the vibrator across the outside folds. "—in and out of my pussy, are you?"

"No," he said. "I'm saying it because I want to be the one to stick that in and out of your pussy. Not to mention doing all the other things that people do when they date. While fully clothed."

"Are we a couple now?" Liz teased him by sliding closer to the camera so he got a good look at her pretty pink lips, glistening with excitement.

"If you insist," he said. His cock was begging to be set free, aching to sink into that sweet, hot flesh.

She sprawled back on the pillow, arching so he got a good view of the vibrator as she pushed it deep. He could see every sweet sway of her hips as she pleasured herself.

"You're so beautiful," he whispered.

"Sean," she cried out. "It feels so good. But it's not enough. I want you inside me. You're thicker and harder than this piece of plastic." Her hand was pumping in a frenzy.

Sean was riveted by her. His mouth was dry and he swallowed compulsively, wanting to lick his way up her stomach. Then he'd hold her wrists above her head and fuck her until she clamped her inner muscles around his cock and milked it dry.

Liz's hips bucked up and down while he admired the curve of her legs and ass. She covered her face with a pillow and turned the vibrator up so high, he could hear the buzz through the computer's speakers. There was a muffled scream as the orgasm shook through her.

"Oh," Liz sat up, the toy still inside her. Her cheeks were flushed, her eyes glazed. Her red, red mouth parted. "I wish you were here to fuck me."

"What's your address?" he growled.

Her eyes went wide. "You'd take a taxi across the city at this hour just to fuck me?"

"I'd take a plane around the world," Sean vowed.

Liz took the toy out and licked it. "Want a taste?" She offered it to him like a lollipop.

Sean nodded.

"I think I'm going to use my fingers this time," Liz leaned back again. "Watch closely now. You wouldn't want to miss a trick."

This time, he did shuck off his pants. Tossing his shirt over his head, he wished she'd open her eyes and see him naked. He took his cock out and pulled on it.

"Do you know what I'm thinking about?" she asked him, her voice a seductive purr.

"I can't imagine," he said, stroking himself in quick yanks.

"You throwing me across this bed and having your way with me."

"I'd like that," he said, staring at her nimble fingers as they toyed with her silky folds and hard bud. "Seeing and hearing you come. Knowing that it's my cock you're imagining inside you."

She opened up one eye and gasped when she saw him. "Oh Sean, I'm supposed to be the tease."

"After dinner," he grunted out. "On Saturday. I'm coming home with you."

"Yes." Her fingers flickered quicker. "Yes," she hissed out.

His cock was primed. The hungry look in her eye driving him closer to the edge. "I'm going to fuck you. I'm going to be rough. You'd like that, right?"

Her head nodded and her hips squirmed.

"A fast fuck, first, to take the edge off, and then again, oh so slow," Sean promised her.

Her fingers were a blur. Liz was gasping little moans with each stroke.

"And then we're going to take a hot shower and soap each other up."

She was shuddering now. He could hear the wetness in every motion of her fingers. "Coming, coming, oh!" Her voice grew louder with each syllable.

He went off first, coating his hand and the camera before he could move away.

Liz followed, her breath coming in short jerky gasps.

"And then we're going to do it all over again," he vowed.

"Promise?" Liz asked, miming licking the cum off his screen.

He leaned back in his seat and let her look her fill. She didn't realize at this angle he could see down her vest. She filled it out nicely. Sean hoped she would let him kiss her chest. He wanted to love every inch of her.

Love? Jesus.

He covered his eyes with his hand and groaned. He had it bad.

"What's the matter?" she asked.

"Nothing. Everything. I wish I'd met you years ago."

"Everything happens for a reason." She leaned back on the pillows and propped herself up on her elbow.

"I used to think so," Sean said, coming as close to honesty as he dared. "But I don't know anything for sure anymore. Maybe there isn't a rhyme or reason to anything. Maybe life is one big random occurrence? Jacques Monod, a French biologist, called it the postulate of objectivity."

"It sounds like you could use a glass of wine." She traced her fingers over the sparkling gem in her belly ring. He'd like to drink champagne off her body. Heck, who was he kidding? He just wanted his mouth all over her.

"I could use a lot of them," Sean sighed, wishing she was in his bed right now instead of on his computer screen.

"I'd share, but I drank most of the bottle before our call." Liz smiled sheepishly. "I was a little nervous."

"Of what? Me?" Sean couldn't imagine her afraid of anything, certainly not him. Didn't she know she had him wrapped around her little finger?

"Yes, you," she said. "I didn't know how you would react when I told you about Jonathan."

"What did you expect?"

Liz shrugged. "I figured you'd find a way to get off the call and then run for the hills."

"Not a chance. I like kids," he said. "The kinky show wasn't necessary. But I loved it." He indicated his cock, still half erect on his stomach.

"I still have some self-esteem issues, too."

"You won't when I get through with you." Sean promised.

"I wondered if you'd find me sexy without my big breasts bouncing around." She pointed to her chest. He wouldn't mind exploring there with his hands and tongue, but she seemed very sensitive about it.

"I'll prove it," he said. "Take off the vest."

"What?" Liz bolted upright, clutching the V-neck opening. "Are you crazy?"

"What do you have to lose?"

"That look." She pointed at him. "That look in your eyes that tells me I'm a sexy love goddess. If you saw my chest, all that would change. At best, I'd get pity. At worst, you'd be turned off."

"Or you could see that I still think you're beautiful."

"Have you ever seen what a double mastectomy looks like?" Liz challenged him.

"No," he admitted.

"Google it. Look up non-reconstructed and reconstructed. We'll talk on Saturday."

She turned off Skype, essentially hanging up on him.

Well, that went well . . . not.

Chapter Eight

"How many computers do you need?" Mike said, bustling into the office and flopping on the couch. He was one of the other teaching assistants.

"How many ya got?" Sean said without looking up from the user interface for the college's mainframe. The mainframe was running through a series of algorithms comparing the drug use for employees of varied professions. Sean had spent most of the last few months painstakingly entering the data he culled from his research. Now it was just a matter of the computer processing the information, looking for statistical correlations. While it did that, Sean tried to get organized. His personal laptop was on his lap and he was deleting the junk mail in his inbox. His work laptop was currently holding down term papers because he had opened the window to get some fresh air.

"You going to be leaving soon?"

"Yeah, I'm leaving in a minute." Content with the mainframe's speed and calculations, Sean turned to look at Mike who was lying down with his arm over his eyes. He wished it was Liz.

"Well, hurry up," Mike said. "You're not the only one who needs to get some crap done. I figured no one would be around today."

"Take it easy. I'm heading down to Queens." Sean shoved his paperwork into his backpack.

"How are things going at the clinic?" Mike said, stifling a yawn.

Sean stood and stretched, rolling out the kinks in his neck. "Gladys and I are meeting today."

"Good luck with that." Mike hauled himself up and into the seat Sean had vacated. "What's this shit?" He tapped the mainframe.

"Leave it alone. It's thinking. If it finishes while you're still here, can you email me the results?"

Mike gave him a thumbs up. "Will do."

Sean packed up his things, secured his backpack straps, and took off at a jog. It felt good to work the kinks out of his muscles. He made good time getting to the subway station and was able to grab a water and eat a PowerBar before the next train.

His luck held and he got a seat while the F train rattled its way beneath the city. Sean got off a stop before the clinic so he could fit in some more exercise. Unfortunately, that made him five minutes late for his meeting.

"I'm sorry," he said to Gladys. "I should have at least picked up coffee."

"It's all right. I was running behind anyway. I just want to touch base with you. How's everything going?"

He sank down into the comfy chair and stared at her Peter Max painting. It was a psychedelic butterfly with lots of heads. It's how he pictured an acid trip would look. "As well as can be expected. I'm having some trouble with the kids who don't want to take me up on the after-school boxing sessions."

"You excel at reaching kids through physical activity. But not all kids are going to respond to that. You need to work on your conversational approach. You're not a good talker."

"Thanks," he said.

Gladys laughed. "Dr. Krauss and I are very pleased with your work. It's just something to think about. You can be too direct. Sometimes

you have to sit back and let it all unfold. But that kills you to do that."
She held up her fists. "You're a man of action."

"Stop," Sean held up his hands in surrender. "My ego can't take it.
If I wanted an analysis of what I'm doing wrong with my life, I'd call
my father."

"You know what Freud said about that?" Gladys raised an eyebrow.

"That 'sometimes a cigar is just a cigar'?" he returned.

"Speaking of cigars, when are you going to bring McManus around
here?" She batted her eyelashes. "I'd like to get to know him better."

Sean made a face. "Dear Lord, why? He thinks using Irish Spring
soap is getting all gussied up. You want to know him better? Go to the
gym. You'll be running back here after five minutes."

"I was hoping to get him out of his environment."

"Good luck with that."

"So what's your plan for reaching the kids who don't like boxing?"

Sean shook his head. "I've been trying to wrap my brain around it.
They need something that will show quick results; otherwise I'll lose
them."

"What about computer sessions?" Gladys gestured at the two laptops he carried in his backpack. "Maybe your non-jocks would get into
computer classes instead. Teach them some job skills instead of beating
each other over the head."

Sean sat up straight in his chair. "That's a great idea."

"All those kids are obsessed with social media now; show them how
to do their own animated pictures or the cartoon with the grumpy cat
and a funny saying or something."

"Maybe not the gifs or memes."

"I love it when you talk nerdy to me," she joked.

"But building a website or a nice blog might be a good way to focus
their energies into something productive." His phone vibrated and he
saw a text from Liz come through.

"Good," Gladys said. "Anything else bothering you?"

Liz.

Sean looked over his shoulder. "Let me close the door."

"This ought to be good."

Sean closed the door and sat back down. "Have you ever dealt with a woman who came to you for therapy about a double mastectomy?"

Gladys sobered. "Oh yes, it's very traumatic. As if the damned cancer wasn't enough, they had to lose their breasts, too. It's very much like the five stages of grief. Why do you ask? Surely one of your kids isn't going through this."

"No," Sean said, glancing at the message from Liz. She was confirming the time he was meeting her and her friends at Angelica Kitchen in the East Village tonight. They had decided to do casual instead of a formal dinner after Liz didn't like the vegetarian choices at the restaurant Sarah had picked out. "I've got a new friend who had it done a year ago," he said. "And I was trying to understand what she went through."

"Did you ask her?"

"I didn't want to pry or put her on the spot."

Gladys rolled her eyes. "Men. If she doesn't want to talk about it, she'll tell you. What have you noticed about her when she does speak of the surgery?"

"She's very self-deprecating."

"It's a hit to the self-esteem."

"But she's absolutely gorgeous," Sean protested.

"A friend, huh?" Gladys waggled her eyebrows at him.

"Maybe a little more than that," he admitted.

Gladys clasped a hand to her heart. "Say it ain't so. All those coeds are going to cry their little hearts off when OMG O'Malley is taken off the market."

Sean rolled his eyes at the nickname. He made the mistake of jogging to school one day, thinking he'd change in the TA office. Almost overnight he went from being unnoticed to being chased around by freshmen. "As long as they stop leaving me little love notes."

"I still say you should sell those to *Penthouse*."

Sean shook his head. "I think that would only encourage them."

"You're probably right." Gladys got up from her desk. "Well, we've got work to do. I just wanted to check in and make sure you didn't need any help."

"I appreciate it." He meant it, too. Dr. Krauss and Gladys had taken him under their wing. He was hoping they were grooming him to come into the practice. But if that wasn't in the cards, it was still a good place to get in the hours needed for his certification.

He'd be glad when he finally got the degree. All the running back and forth from here to campus was killing him.

✳✳✳ ✳✳✳

Angelica Kitchen was a cute little place with really good food. Sean had eaten a big lunch in anticipation of being hungry later, but he had been wrong. The portions were large and savory.

The four of them sat at a table, their knees practically touching, but it was a homey feel, even with all the other patrons bustling around. The soft murmur of voices washed over the music playing in the background. It was a chill place, one he wouldn't have ever gone to on his own.

He held Liz's hand under the table while they waited for their coffee and desserts. Sarah and Cole turned out to be regular people. He had been a little overwhelmed when he realized just who they were. Sarah, of course, was the famous porn star Sugar. And Cole was the scion of an old money Manhattan family. The Cannings were well known philanthropists and, although their reputation took a hit when Cole married a retired adult film actress, they seemed to be bouncing back by ignoring her past. Baby Christopher, who was with his grandparents tonight, certainly helped. And judging by the photos, he was the apple of his grandparents' eyes.

"I've been looking for a place to train," Cole said. "Tell me more about this gym you belong to."

Yeah, like a hoi polloi would ever come down to McManus's gym to work out. He'd take one look at the place and have his driver take him uptown as fast as traffic would allow. Still, Cole seemed a lot more down to earth than his reputation made him out to be.

The waitress delivered their chicory coffee and four dessert plates. Sean was stuffed, but he wasn't about to let the confections go to waste.

"McManus used to coach for Team USA about twenty years ago, then he decided to open his own place." Sean poured almond milk into his coffee. "He's got a good eye for talent, but knows how to bring out the best in any fighter."

"Sounds like someone I'd like to meet," Cole said, stirring raw sugar into his.

"Let me know and I'll come down with you and give you an introduction." They bumped fists. "But I'm warning you, he's a real prick if he thinks you aren't working up to your potential—your potential being whatever he wants it to be."

"Liz tells me you work with troubled youth," Sarah said, and forked a piece of pineapple cake in her mouth.

"What?" Sean blurted out. *Did she know?*

"At the gym." Liz gave him a quizzical look.

"Oh, right. Yeah. They're good kids; they just need something to focus on that builds up their self-esteem."

"Aren't you afraid they're going to take what you've taught them and beat up other kids at school?" Sarah's tone was questioning and not accusatory, but Sean had heard that argument before.

"If they want to stay in my program, they wouldn't dare. And anyway, most of these kids already know how to beat the shit out of someone. I'm teaching them a sport and a code. You don't start a fight. You avoid a fight. But if you can't avoid a fight, you end the fight."

"Amen," Cole said.

"Some of Sean's pupils are girls," Liz added, exchanging a glance with Sarah. "Wouldn't you have liked to be able to knock the crap out of some asshole who was touching you and forcing you into a corner?"

"Definitely," Sarah admitted. "So, are you going to teach Jonathan how to box?"

"If he wants to," Sean said at the same time Liz said, "He's too young."

"No he's not." Sean smiled at her. "But it's your call."

"Isn't it dangerous?" Liz nibbled her lip and Sean wanted those pretty white teeth on him.

"Not at all." He snapped himself out of his lustful thoughts. *Soon.* "With the equipment we have them use and how we set up the practice bouts."

"We'll see," she said.

"When my mom said that, it usually meant no."

"Well, when I say that, it means I'll have to look into it more." Liz jostled her shoulder into his.

"You're welcome to come down to the gym, too. Bring Jonathan. Just let me know ahead of time and I can set a few things up."

"Do you spar?" Cole asked.

Sean nodded. "McManus is trying to get me to be a punching bag for this guy, Kyle Donovan. He's going to be big. But he hits like a freight train."

"We should go a couple of rounds," Cole said, but it wasn't a challenge. More like, let's knock a few back.

"I'd like that." Sean took a bite of his dessert, a raspberry rhubarb tart.

"Women bond over shopping," Sarah told her husband.

"Men bond over beer and sports," he shot back.

"I'll go easy on you," Sean said with a straight face.

"Oh, them's fightin' words."

Sarah made exaggerated sniffing sounds. "The testosterone in here is choking."

They laughed and went back to devouring their desserts.

"So is it dangerous for you?" Liz said, when they were finishing up their coffees. "The boxing?"

"It depends on the opponent. McManus runs a tight ship. He doesn't want anyone hurt. None of the guys I know will go out of the way to put you in the hospital, but there's always a risk in the heat of the moment. Sometimes you walk into a punch or take it the wrong way. Shit happens. But not as much as you think. Remember, we're wearing head gear, gloves, and a mouthguard. If I was Donovan's sparring partner, I'd wear a chest protector to soak up the impact on my ribs."

"Why would you want to get beat up?" Liz shuddered.

"Thanks for the vote of confidence," Sean said and chuckled with the rest of them. "Money. If you can take the hit, you get paid for it. It's expensive living in New York City."

"A little like porn, only not as messy?" Liz nodded as if she was understanding something.

"Excuse me?" he choked on his coffee.

"You like boxing. It seems like easy money, so you go for it."

Sean blinked. Was that what Mary Katherine thought? Easy money for something she'd do for free. His brain tried to shut down at the thought of his sister having sex, but the scientist in him had to put the facts on the table. Okay, so he got why she stripped and understood cringingly why she had gone into porn. The only other factor was the drugs. Looking at Cole and Sarah, it didn't appear that they were users.

He could see Sarah lighting up a joint or maybe Cole doing a line of coke, but they weren't addicts.

"Have I offended you?" Liz asked, nudging him.

"No," he said. "I just never thought of it that way. It's interesting. My mind was taking the metaphor even further."

"He said metaphor," Liz fluttered her hands. "My English lit heart is beating pitter pat."

"Ha," Sarah said. "Except now, it's your psychologist's heart."

"What?" Sean said.

"Thanks for spoiling the surprise," Liz huffed at Sarah, exasperated. "I was going to tell you later so we could celebrate with a bottle of champagne. I enrolled in NYU."

"You did?" His lips felt numb, but he forced them to crack a smile.

"Silver campus. Maybe we'll have some classes together."

"This is so cute, I want to barf." Sarah giggled and threw her arm around her husband.

"What classes are you taking?"

Please not Intro to Social Work. Please not . . .

"The only one I've had time to think about is Intro to Psych, but I'm wait-listed."

Sweat broke out on Sean's forehead. The restaurant narrowed to a tiny tunnel for a moment. He gulped down the last of his coffee, trying to quell the panic. It wasn't a class he was teaching. But what if she heard about OMG O'Malley?

"You all right?" Cole asked.

He gave the other man a tight nod.

"It starts next semester," Liz sipped the last of her apricot kanten. "Do you think they'll let us know if we get in before the first day of class, or should I just show up and wait for them to kick me out?"

"Uh, usually, they open up another class if the wait-list is too long."

"Oh, good." Liz brightened.

"You'll probably get an email letting you know what's going on soon."

He was a dead man. There was no way around this. He was going to have to tell her soon. He didn't want her to find out from someone else. Sean stared up toward the front of the restaurant when a familiar face caught his eye.

Sabrina?

She didn't seem shocked to see him. Crooking her little finger at him, she walked toward the bathrooms.

"Excuse me." Sean got up. "I'm going to hit the little boys' room." He prayed that Cole wouldn't follow and, as luck would have it, he didn't. Sean made his way to the restaurant's bathrooms where Sabrina was waiting with her shoulder hitched up against the wall. Luckily, the lines were long enough that he could have a conversation without attracting attention.

"Are you following me?" he asked in a low voice, aware of the people in line listening.

Sabrina just shrugged. At least she was sober, her eyes clear and bright.

"You could have called my cell phone."

"I wanted to see your face when I gave you this." Sabrina handed him a folded piece of paper.

Raising an eyebrow, he opened it.

Next Saturday, 10 a.m. 45th and Lexington, Tower Hotel, Suite 2245. Bring STD results.

"And this is?" Sean let a bunch of men go ahead of him so he could continue talking to Sabrina

"Your debut. I vouched for you. If you can prove you're clean, you're in."

"In for what?"

Sabrina framed her fingers and angled them toward his face. "You oughta be in pictures."

"I don't believe this," he said.

"'You want answers? You want the truth?'" She barked out her best Colonel Jessup impersonation from *A Few Good Men*. "You can't handle the truth."

"I'll be there," he said, just to shut her up.

There was no way in hell he was going to go through with it, but maybe he would go to the hotel and see for himself if they were handing out pills like M&Ms.

"You better." Sabrina got out of line and pulled the brim of her hat down over her head. "I put my neck out for you."

"Why?" he asked, following her back to the main part of the restaurant.

"Desiree. She wouldn't want you to be so tortured."

"I'm not tortured." But he was talking to her back. She waggled her fingers at him over her shoulder but didn't turn around.

Chapter Nine

Leaving Sean in her apartment while she walked Mrs. Ritter back home, Liz listened to her neighbor with half an ear.

Jonathan was an angel.

He went to bed right away without an argument.

Yeah, right.

Liz would bet her last nickel that when she went to check on him, he'd have a flashlight and a comic book under the covers. Still, tomorrow was Sunday. They could sleep in.

She wondered if Sean would be staying.

"Thanks again," she said to Mrs. Ritter, standing guard at her door so none of the cats got out.

"Any time, dear." The older woman stifled a yawn behind her hand and Liz felt a little guilty they had gotten back so late.

"Why don't you come up for brunch tomorrow, around ten?" Liz asked.

"That sounds lovely. Is there anything I can bring?"

"Just yourself. Goodnight."

Liz ran a mental checklist through her head. She had enough to make Belgian waffles. She'd send Sean to get strawberries in the morning. Stopping at her own door, she wondered if she wanted to introduce her lover to her son this way. As soon as she introduced them, Mrs. Ritter started mentally measuring Sean for a wedding tux. What would she think when she saw him over Liz's breakfast table? She sighed and opened the door.

Sean was pacing. He had been distracted ever since he came back from the bathroom at the restaurant.

"Are you okay?" she asked. "We don't have to do this, if you don't want. If you're not in the mood. I don't want to force anything."

"I got some disturbing news at dinner," he said. "About my sister. My head's all messed up. I'm afraid I'm not good company right now. I just don't want you to think I'm bailing on you because your friends scared me off or something. They're nice. I like them. They're real protective of you."

"They liked you, too. Wait until you meet the rest of the bunch. It's like one big crazy family." Liz's heart sunk. He was leaving.

"I wish I wasn't so torn up inside. She was my big sister. I looked up to her, and I can't believe she's dead. I feel like such a failure because she didn't reach out to me for help if she was in trouble."

She walked over and took his hand. "When's the last time you talked to her?"

"About a few weeks before she died," he said, looking down at their joined hands. Sean stroked his thumb across her knuckles.

It did things to her, but she had to take a deep breath and concentrate. She'd jump his bones later. Right now, he needed a friend. "What did she say?"

Sean shook his head. "Not much. The usual. She loved her job. She had a new roommate who she hated. I wanted to get together for lunch or dinner. She said sure. But we never nailed down plans." He took a shuddering breath.

"Come on, sit down with me. Why don't I put on some coffee?"

"I'm too jittery for coffee." He pulled her into his arms for a back-cracking hug. "Things are happening. Things that I didn't expect. I've got to tell you something, but I just can't get the words out."

"You're scaring me," Liz said.

He immediately released her. "I'm sorry. I'm in a bad place right now. I should go."

"Wait, let's put on a movie and just relax on the couch. No emotional upheaval. No life or death situations. Just you and me and some alone time."

Some of his tension eased out of his shoulders. "I'd like that."

"Sit," she pointed. "I'll get a bottle of wine."

When she came back, he had kicked off his shoes and sat with his feet up on her frayed ottoman. He looked so natural there, so at home. The clinking of the wine glasses gave her presence away and he opened his eyes.

"Sorry for freaking out."

"I've been there," she said, setting up a TV table and putting the wine and glasses on it. "Are you hungry?"

"God, no," he said, rubbing his stomach. "I didn't think vegetarian food would fill me up, but that was a great dinner."

"And healthy," she added.

"I still like meat."

"I understand." Liz sat down next to him and clicked on the television. "What are you in the mood for?"

He curled his arm around her shoulders. "You pick. I just like being here with you."

"Do you want to talk more about your sister?"

"Liz, it's the last thing I want to do." His eyes were so soulful and apologetic, she kissed his forehead.

"You got it."

She found an old comedy on one of the movie channels, something mindless and entertaining. Liz got the impression he was still lost in his thoughts during most of the movie, but he traced patterns on her shoulders, periodically kissing the top of her head. Liz was snuggled next to him, nuzzling his neck from time to time.

Liz couldn't remember who kissed who first, but she was soon wrapped in Sean's arms and they were sucking face like teenagers. *God, he can kiss.* Cupping his face, she eased up on the deep, drugging, tongue kisses to look into his eyes.

"I want to be your fantasy," she purred.

"You already are," Sean said, bringing her down for another kiss.

"We . . . should . . . take . . . this into the bedroom," Liz gasped out between kisses.

"Not tonight," he said. "There's not enough time."

"We can be quick," she tugged his shirt loose from his pants. "Save the slow round for later. But if I don't have you tonight, I will go insane."

He scooted away from her and knelt in front of the couch. Touching her knee, Sean smoothed his hand up her soft wool skirt. She had dressed with him in mind tonight. Everything from her baby blue cashmere thrift-store sweater to the short black skirt was made to be tossed off with minimal fuss.

"Leave the boots on," he begged, tugging on the corner of her panties.

As long as he let her keep her shirt on, Liz thought.

"These are the same ones you wore for me on Wednesday."

"You noticed the boots?"

He licked up one until he came to the top and then he gently bit the inside of her thigh. Liz opened her knees to allow him to continue the nibbling trail. Fumbling with her skirt, she bunched it high on her waist to give him more room.

"Your panties are a little more sensible than the other night." Of course, she wore a strip of fabric the other night. These were pink, delicate, and sexy as hell. He traced the lace edge with his tongue.

"More comfortable too." She ran her fingers through that glorious mess of dark hair.

"You can't be comfortable in these." He ran his finger up the middle of them. "Sopping wet." He took her panties in his hands and ripped them open.

"Oh," she cried. Moaning as Sean dipped his fingers inside her heat, Liz eased her head back. She raised her hips to accept the penetration as he slipped another finger inside her.

"Keep looking at me like that," Sean asked. "I want to see your pretty face when you start to come."

He kissed the side of her knee, darted his tongue over the back of it. She tried to force her legs closed against the delicious sensations he was causing, but Sean wouldn't allow it. The slow press of his fingers wasn't enough, and she rode them, trying to catch the elusive pinnacle, which was just out of reach.

Sean thumbed over her soaked pearl, then leaned in and sucked on the hard bud. Liz clamped down on his fingers as her body shuddered to climax. Lapping up the wetness, he didn't relent with his fingers.

She gripped his head, forcing him to look up at her. "I thought you wanted to watch," she panted.

"Next time." He grinned and went back to licking.

Her fingers tangling in his hair, she watched him drench his face as his tongue continued to hit her sensitive spots. "If you don't get up and take me to bed right now, I swear I will fuck you on the floor."

"Do something," he mocked.

He did not know who he was messing with.

Liz tackled him back and they rolled on the floor laughing. They bumped into the table and the wine bottle just missed their heads by inches as it fell. The glasses fell to the carpet too, but luckily nothing broke.

Liz made short work of his jeans and straddled him. His thick heat at last slid into her and she tightened her core around him. Pressing him flat on his back, she made sure to take her sweet time lowering herself up and down his thick hard length.

"Finally," she moaned.

"Finally," he gasped, his hands gripping her thighs.

She watched the lazy satisfaction in his face turn to yearning hunger. He grasped her hips and held her to him while he lifted himself deeper. The hard slap of their bodies slamming together was loud in the apartment.

Tossing her head, Liz rode him, using her leg and thigh muscles to give them both the best angle. His cock stretched her. He was nice and long, going deep when she sat astride him, holding still so she could just enjoy him being inside her. He held her there when she would have moved. Deep, so damned deep . . .

"Stay there," he whispered, reaching his fingers for her clit.

She guided him to the correct spot and bounced on him again.

Sean gritted his teeth. His body trembled below her and tensed.

"That's it, Sean. It's your turn."

His fingers jerked out of rhythm. Warmth flooded her. His body sagged and a primal groan of satisfaction left him. Liz collapsed on top of him, eager for more of his kisses.

"I warned you," she said.

"I never listen." Sean held her tight. "I think I have rug burns on my ass."

"Better you than me."

She listened to the racing of his heartbeat and stayed clasped to him until it returned to a slower rhythm. She was getting a chill on her backside, but it was worth it for a few more of those kisses—and his fingers stroking her into another quick orgasm.

"Are you ready for that shower?" he asked after she whimpered her release.

"Not unless I can leave my top on," she said, raising herself up on her elbow.

"I Googled the pictures."

Liz looked away.

"No, damn it." Sean turned her chin back so she was facing him. "I wish I had been there to help you through the horrifying experience. But you are so fucking strong, you didn't need me."

"I had a lot of help."

"Doesn't lessen the fact that you are the most beautiful, most caring, bravest, and fiercest woman I have ever met. I want to kiss every inch of you. But not until you're ready."

"Could be a while," she said.

"I've got time." He smoothed his hand over her ass.

"I think I'm going to get my nipples tattooed."

His hand stopped. "Um, what are you going to get? Stars? Hearts?"

She thumped him in the chest. "I'm going to get nipples tattooed on the reconstructed breasts."

"Why?" he asked.

"So they look normal."

"Oh, I didn't know they did that."

"You didn't look too hard at the mastectomy pictures, did you?" Liz kissed his cheek. "It explained all that."

"I'll go back and do more research."

"I think you just like looking at boobs."

Sean shrugged. "I like the real thing better."

"I used to be the real thing," she said. "Those puppies were natural. Now, not so much."

He lifted her up under the armpits so her chest was in his face.

"What are you doing?" Liz started to struggle, then froze.

Sean placed a chaste kiss through her sweater on each side of her chest. She didn't feel it, not in the usual way. But she had to clench her jaw as tears threatened. He gently rolled her off him and stood up, fixing his pants. Offering her his hand, he said. "I've got to get going."

Liz stared at his hand and then reached out to take it. Didn't he know that he completely knocked her world off its axis with those two sweet kisses? She let him pull her to her feet.

"I wish I could stay here tonight." He murmured into her temple.

"You can."

"I'm going to be tossing and turning all night. I also don't want Jonathan to meet me like that. Not the first time. Can you bring him by the gym this week? Wednesday?"

"Sure," she said. "I'm still not convinced about the boxing, but it's a date. Know a good pizza place around there?"

"Yeah, I'll set it up."

He swooped her back for another kiss that lasted until her toes were tingling again. "We still need to have a long talk. Maybe tomorrow night. I know you probably won't be able to get away, but we can talk on the phone."

"Or you can come here. Jonathan is asleep by nine."

Sean cupped her face in his hand. "I'd like that."

"See you tomorrow." Liz walked him to the door.

He crushed her to him one last time and left her breathless from the passion of his kiss.

"What was that for?" She touched her lips, still throbbing from the pleasure of his mouth.

"Just in case." He kissed her forehead.

Liz stared at the door a long time after he left. When she snapped out of it, she realized she hadn't invited him to the FATE meeting on Monday.

Chapter Ten

After a quick trip to the market, Liz and Jonathan made up a batch of Belgian waffles with blueberries and served them to Mrs. Ritter along with some veggie sausages. It was a busy morning, but also a fun one. After brunch, she took Jonathan to the park and then they walked to the comic book store to pick up the newest Spiderman.

While Jonathan loafed on the couch, Liz finished up some client work she had been putting off. She updated the taxidermist's website and sent him an invoice. Feeling accomplished, she started to tackle the school's Halloween fundraiser. Judith and Chloe were finally on the same page. Judith wanted the poster to be scary and Chloe wanted it tasteful. After much back and forth, they decided to have a skeleton holding a jack-o-lantern on one side and a kitty cat (Chloe's words) wearing a black witch's hat on the opposite side. Liz could work with that. She filled in the dates and the times and the RSVP number for the dance and began to work on the skeleton. If she had been pressed for time, Liz would have gone for a stock photo.

Part of the fun, though, was getting to be creative and practice her drawing skills. It was nice to use another part of her brain. She had picked up the Intro to Psychology textbook and it was a doozy. Maybe she could study with Sean. Liz would have to ask him about classes.

"Baby?" she called out.

"I'm not a baby," came the aggravated answer.

"Do you want a glass of almond milk?"

"No," Jonathan droned.

"Can I talk to you for a moment?"

"Sure," he sighed loudly. With great theatrics, he put down his comic and came over to her desk. "I cleaned my room."

"Stuffing things under the bed isn't cleaning, but that's not what I want to talk to you about."

"Okay." He snuggled up to her.

She hugged him until he shimmied away. "That's cool." He pointed at her screen.

"It's for your school. They're having a dance party on Halloween. I've got to design the raffle tickets too and then I'll be all done."

And then I can get back to my paying gigs.

Liz tried not to sigh at her inbox. She was a little backed up, but it beat the alternative. The design work came in waves, so she had to scurry like a hamster on the wheel so she could put food on the table when everyone was ordering through Vistaprint instead of with her.

"Can I go back to my comic now?" Jonathan asked, shifting from one foot to the other.

"Not just yet. I wanted to let you know that Mama has met someone." Liz braced herself for the torrent of questions.

"You meet a lot of people." Jonathan yawned.

So much for him making this easy on me.

"I mean, I met someone I like very much. His name is Sean." Liz wondered how much detail she should go into. Should she say, *we're dating?* Or *he's my boyfriend?* Or just stick with *friend?*

"Okay," Jonathan shrugged. He spotted one of his troll pencils sticking out of her cup. He snatched it and twirled the pencil until the little troll sitting on the eraser had fully experienced a bad hair day.

Liz wasn't sure she was getting through to him. "We're going to meet Sean on Wednesday after school."

"Where?" He looked up from the troll.

At last some interest.

"At a gym he belongs to."

"Okay," he shrugged again.

"I want you to let me know how you feel about all this." Liz held him by the shoulders so he'd look at her. "If you don't like him or if this situation feels weird to you, let me know. You are the most important thing in my life. I love you so very much."

"Mo-om," he whined. "I know that. You tell me all the time."

"I don't want you to forget it. Fine, go back to your comic."

"Thank you."

Well, that was easier than she thought it would be.

But she knew Jonathan would be thinking about her words and percolating what had been said. The conversation had gone better than she expected. She was glad he wasn't feeling threatened by another male in her life.

Liz fiddled with the skeleton until she got it perfect and then saved her work. A knock on the door startled her and she looked up.

"I'll get it!" Jonathan cried and he ran toward the door.

Was it Sean? She smoothed her hand over her hair and wished she was wearing something other than a Ramones T-shirt and yoga pants.

"Who is it?" Liz said as Jonathan stood on tippy toes to see out the peephole.

"No one."

"All right, back away." It was probably just the wind or maybe one of her neighbors had dropped something off for her.

When she opened the door, there wasn't anyone there, but a DVD case that had been propped up on the door fell back on the doorstop.

"Cool, a movie!"

Liz's hand shot out and grabbed Jonathan's shoulder before he could dive for it. "Go to your room," she said, placing her body between him and the door.

"But, Mom? What did I do?"

"Nothing, sweet boy. Nothing. Just please. Go to your room."

"Fine." He shook free of her arm and stalked off.

His door slammed and she couldn't blame him. Bending down, she picked up the DVD and cradled it to her chest. Liz ran to the stairwell and looked down, but she didn't see anyone. She didn't even hear anyone on the steps.

"Hello?" Her voice echoed and the feeling of isolation hit her. Hurrying back into her apartment, she closed the door.

Lucky Number Seven

There she was on the cover, on her hands and knees. The title of the DVD covering her nipples and not much else. Steve was inside of her, but all you could see of him was his torso above her moon-shaped ass.

Oh, no.

Jonathan almost saw that. Call her old-fashioned, but she didn't want that picture to be the first one he saw of his father. After locking the door with shaking hands, Liz pressed her forehead against the door. Why was this happening now? She darted into her bedroom and opened the case. The disc was there, and a note fluttered and fell to the floor.

Oh, God.

She stuffed the DVD in the bottom of her underwear drawer and bent to pick up the note. Should she call the police? But how seriously would they take it? It was just a DVD left at her door, and then her secret would be out for sure. Damn it, why now? When she was just getting back on track?

Unfolding the note, she read the words.

Oh, shit.

"Mom? Can I come out now?"

"Not just yet, baby." Liz called back, amazed that her voice sounded so normal.

"Am I in trouble?"

"No, honey, I'll explain in a few minutes."

As soon as I get my head together.

She reached for her phone and texted Sean. *I've got to cancel tonight. Something came up.*

Then she dialed Sarah's number.

✳✳✳ ✳✳✳

They met in Central Park's ancient playground so Jonathan could play on the obelisks and pyramids. Sarah brought her an iced coffee with a shot of Jameson in it. They sat shoulder to shoulder on a bench and watched Jonathan play with the other kids. Cole was on Daddy duty, and Sarah was pleased to get out and cut loose for a little bit.

"I still say you should call the cops." Sarah shook the ice in her own drink.

"And say what? There wasn't anything threatening in the note."

"'See you soon?'" Sara turned her head to look at her. "You don't think that's threatening? It's a stalker. And he knows where you live. I want you and Jonathan to come live with us for a week or so until we find out what's going on."

"Absolutely not. For all we know, it's Steve playing one of his dumb games."

"You haven't seen that asshole in nine years. He had a hard enough time finding his dick in his pants. There's no way he could have tracked you down in New York. For what? To finally meet his son? No, my money is on that tabloid guy."

"Then why leave the video? Why not just wait outside the walk-up and take pictures of me going to and from work?"

"Maybe he has," Sarah said ominously.

"Oh, crap." Liz started texting the other FATE members. "I'm canceling tomorrow's meeting. The last thing any of us need is a tabloid reporter in our faces."

"Okay, calm down. Don't get paranoid."

"You're the one telling me to move in with you," Liz said.

"Look, let's say it is this tabloid shithead. What's his name?"

"Ricky Rose."

"Really?" Sarah drawled, sucking the last bit of doctored coffee down.

"You've never read the *Rose By Any Other Name* blog? He's got a radio show too at one of the indie stations. I've never tuned in."

"Maybe you should start. Besides, if it is Ricky, he's got to be bored sick. You take Jonathan to school. Have a coffee. Walk back home to work. And then go pick him up. Yawn."

"Thanks, we can't all be international bestselling authors jetting off to whatever island your husband's family owns."

In the hurt silence that followed, Liz felt awful.

"I'm sorry. I didn't mean that. I'm a nasty bitch."

Sarah put her arm around her shoulder and squeezed. "I'm just worried about you. I don't want what happened to me to happen to you."

Sarah's former manager Martin Levine was currently doing time for attempted murder after stalking and attacking her all because she dared to retire from porn and move to New York.

"Nobody cares that much."

At Sarah's sharp look, Liz elaborated. "I mean, if that was going to happen, it would have happened a long time ago. Right now, I'm what you described. A work-at-home mom of a pre-tween, who survived cancer by getting her breasts removed. Who wants to stalk that?"

"I hate when you talk about yourself like that. Have you told Sean yet?"

"No, I don't want him to worry."

"I want him to worry." Sarah rooted around in her purse for some change. "I'm going to get a can of soda. Wait right here."

Liz peeked inside Sarah's open purse and saw the fifth of Jameson. She took a big sip of her own iced coffee. She had to admit; it settled her nerves and evened things out a bit.

Pouring the cola into her empty iced coffee cup, Sarah handed it to her to hold while she put the can in the recycling bin. When she came back, she angled her body to shield what she was doing, and she dumped a healthy dollop of whiskey into the cup.

"I hear alcoholics do this," Liz said. "Drinking in the park on Sunday afternoons."

Jonathan was on a swing, kicking himself higher and higher. Liz fretted that he was going to flip over the top bar of the swing set.

"Ease up, sweetheart," she called to him.

"We could have done this at a bar, what's the difference?" Sarah tightened the cap and secured the bottle in her purse.

"Well, considering this isn't New Orleans, I'm pretty sure this is illegal." Liz unzipped her coat. The mild October breeze cooled her cheeks, which were flushed from the alcohol.

"Oh, lighten up," Sarah said. "It's two drinks. Neither one of us is driving. I wanted something to calm both our nerves."

"I guess if we read about Sugar and Spice drinking together in Central Park tomorrow, we'll know it's Ricky."

"There's a pleasant thought." Sarah looked around. "I don't see anyone paying us any attention. What's this Ricky look like?"

"I can't be sure. He sent me a fake picture. If the picture on his website byline is anything to go by, he's got long blonde hair and glasses."

Sarah took out her phone. "I'm looking him up now." She thumbed through until she found his avatar. Squinting around the park, Sarah shook her head. "I don't see him."

"Maybe he has a telephoto lens?"

Sarah smacked her.

"I know. I'm rattled. The drink helped. I can't stop looking over my shoulder though."

"That's not necessarily a bad thing,"

"'See you soon,'" Liz repeated the message on the note. "What does that mean? Is he coming to the door to visit? Or is it a creepy note to say that I'm being watched."

"Okay, let's look at this rationally. He knows you're Spice. He wants you to know that he knows."

Liz finished her iced coffee and Sarah dumped half her drink into Liz's cup. Liz eyed it. She was going to dump it when Sarah wasn't looking.

Jonathan had moved on to the climbing wall part of the playset. It wasn't too high, but he was having trouble hauling himself over the top to the platform. She was about to go help when a few boys tugged him up and then they slid down the slide one after the other.

"That's all we know," Liz said. "So we're going to have to wait until he makes his next move. And he's not going to do that if I'm staying with you. Maybe I shouldn't have told Sean to stay home tonight."

"And now we get to the good part. Please tell me you took that nice hunk of man in your bed last night."

"The floor, actually," Liz admitted.

Sarah whooped and high-fived her.

"He's got issues, though."

"We all do."

Liz nodded. "I want to him to tell me about his sister, but it's still so raw for him. He got some bad news last night, but he wouldn't tell me about it."

"He'll open up when he's ready. Why don't you text him that your schedule cleared?"

"Well, because tomorrow's a school day and I've got to get ready for the week. This whole 'See you soon' nonsense really put a wrench in my plans."

"If you call him at eleven tonight, he'll think it's a booty call. You don't want to go down that road."

"I'm seeing him on Wednesday, that'll be good enough. He's meeting Jonathan."

"Good, but I still want you to tell him about the DVD."

Liz groaned. "Then he'll feel obligated to come over."

"Why is that a bad thing?" Sarah tapped her cup against Liz's. "Cheers!"

"Because I'm a strong, independent woman . . ."

"Who could really use a little TLC," Sarah finished.

The boys were running around playing freeze tag. Liz smiled at their antics. She was happy Jonathan was having a good time. She worried he was too into his computer games, but she didn't want to take them away unless she had a good reason.

"Speaking of tender loving care," Liz said, "I was wondering if you would come to the plastic surgeon with me?"

Sarah crinkled up her nose. "You're not going to do something drastic like a nose job, are you?"

"I'm going to finally have them tattoo my nipples."

"Ouch."

"Won't feel a thing." Liz tapped her breasts.

A small smile toyed around Sarah's lips. "He must be something."

"I could be doing this for me, you know."

"I know you're doing this for you. But this is the first time you wanted to do something to make you feel sexier. I like that."

The kids had switched to tag. Jonathan was "it." Liz watched her son count to twenty and then take off, following shrieks and giggles. Two years ago, she thought she wouldn't even be sitting here right now. She had asked Sarah to take him if the cancer won. While she didn't die, Liz hadn't really been living either.

"At first, I was waiting for the cancer to come back. It's a motherfucker like that, you know? Just when you think you won— BAM. It's back and it brought friends. But then the first year went by and I thought maybe I could just stay under cancer's radar. Like it's this malevolent ogre under the bridge. If I didn't expect too much, if I didn't chase any big dreams, I could live long enough to see Jonathan grow up."

"Oh, Liz." Sarah gripped her friend's hand. "Why didn't you tell me? You've been so strong for all of us through everything."

"I don't even think I rationalized it this way before. It was subconscious. But chatting online with Sean, trying to keep him at arm's length for three months didn't work. I really like him. And I'm so scared I'm going to fuck it up."

"You *will* fuck it up," Sarah said. "And he'll fuck it up. That's how relationships work."

"He says my surgery won't bother him, but what if it does?" Liz tossed her drink in the trash as the booze was now churning inside her stomach in an unpleasant way. "What if he's so turned off by my chest? I don't want to risk ruining what we have."

"He'll deal. Or you will. Maybe you'll invent a new kink, shirt-wearing sex."

Liz rolled her eyes. "I can handle that."

"You can handle anything. You pretty much *have* handled everything. And now you're going back to school to get your degree, then your therapist license."

"Hold on there, that's a long ways away."

"You'll get there," Sarah said. "With or without that sexy boxer next to you. Or underneath you."

Liz playfully elbow-jabbed her. "Maybe cancer left the DVD. 'See you soon.'"

"Ugh, don't even joke about that."

"Five more minutes!" Liz called to Jonathan.

"I'm in no hurry." Sarah leaned back on the bench. "I may take a nap, however."

"I always start the five-minute routine early. It cuts down on the 'Aw Mom's." Liz hid a yawn. "You had to say 'nap' didn't you?"

"Somebody kept you up last night?"

"Hopefully the same somebody that will keep me up tonight, too." Liz pulled out her phone to text Sean.

"That's my girl."

Chapter Eleven

Sean was back in the teaching assistants' office at the university, trying not to look at the couch and failing. He had a hard-on that even the number crunching wasn't making go down. He lost himself in the mindless task of grading papers so he didn't have to think about Sabrina's offer or how he got a reprieve from telling Liz the truth. When his phone buzzed a text through from her, his cock jumped.

Crisis handled. Can you still come over tonight?

"So much for the reprieve," Sean thought, but he was too excited not to text back:

Eleven o'clock? Should I bring anything?

Her return text came only moments later.

Lube? Body paint? Anal beads? Handcuffs?

Sean groaned aloud. There went the rest of the afternoon. He adjusted himself and texted: *Be ready to be on all fours tonight.*

I'm ready now.

So am I. Don't wear anything . . . complicated.

Do I get to rip your underwear off tonight?

Sean gave a husky laugh. *Who says I'm wearing underwear?*

Did you know I won an AVN award for Best Blow Job?

I did not.

I'll show you how I got it tonight.

Does 10:00 work better for you?

Yes.

"Thank God," he said aloud. Then his conscience hit him, and he typed: *Before all the fun stuff, I've got to tell you something.*

No. After all the fun stuff. Also, J has school tomorrow a.m. Do you mind leaving B4 he gets up?

Not at all.

After dealing all day with a hard-on that never entirely went away, Sean knocked on the door at 9:59 p.m., primed for anything Liz wanted to give him. After a few minutes, he heard Liz disengage the locks and let him in. She was wearing a black silk kimono, tied in a loose knot. It was short, barely covering her knees. Her eyes were outlined to stand out and her lipstick made him want to kiss it off. He leaned in to do so, but she stopped him with a hand on his chest.

"You didn't see anything else out there, did you?" Liz bit her lip and looked around the doorway.

"No, why?"

She pulled him in and locked the door. "Have a seat," she said. "Can I get you a drink?"

"I'm good." He said, liking the way the silk slithered over her bare legs.

"You're better than good." She straddled him on the couch. Liz wasn't wearing anything under the kimono. He slid his hands under the flaps and cupped her ass with both hands, squeezing.

"I've been thinking about this all day." Sean held her against his cock. He felt her heat through his jeans.

She placed fierce, hot kisses on his neck, as she unbuttoned his shirt to get to his T-shirt. "Off," she said, licking along his bottom lip and then nipping it. Sean let her pull off his shirts and leaned back as she buried her face into his neck. Caressing her thighs now, he parted the kimono to reveal the delta between her legs. He maneuvered his fingers between them and searched for her spot.

"Oh no," she said. "Not yet. You make me crazy with your fingers and tongue. It's my turn to drive you wild."

"Are you sure we're all right out here?"

"We should be. He's been out for about an hour and his door is closed. Try not to roar when you come." She darted her tongue in his mouth and he forgot everything except for the hot, lush body grinding into his and the sweet seduction of her kiss.

It wasn't long before she was making little noises against his mouth and rubbing herself against the bulge in his jeans. She was soaking the front of his pants, but he couldn't get enough. The tie in her robe was like a do not cross line, so he touched her everywhere else. He found out she was ticklish behind her knee. That if he raked his short nails across her inner thighs, she moaned.

She came while they were kissing and he held her hips down as she ground into him, shuddering her climax.

"Not how I planned it," she panted. "Just too damned sexy for me." Liz wiggled off his lap.

"No complaints here," he said, kicking off his shoes to let her undress him.

Sean's hands dug into the sofa cushion as he kept a desperate ear out for Jonathan. The kid should be deeply asleep, but if Sean heard that door crack, he was prepared to move fast. Liz popped the first button of his jeans, kissed his abs, and licked down to his waistline.

He lifted his hips so she could ease his pants and underwear down his legs. She wrapped the silk of the kimono around her hand and grasped his cock at the base. Stroking him with her silk-encased hands, Liz darted her tongue around his balls.

"Oh!" he cried out and cursed. He didn't mean to be so loud. "Maybe we should—"

"Fuck in the bedroom?" Liz filled in.

The tip of his cock glistened, and Liz darted her tongue over the beaded wetness.

"Sounds like a plan, but first I'm going to make you come."

Before his brain could even consider an answer to that, her mouth enveloped him, taking him deep. The room was filled with her greedy sucking sounds and the pounding of his heart. The things her tongue was doing to him should be illegal. Sean tried to remember statistics, the periodic table, anything to make this last longer, but Liz's mouth was moving too quickly, the suction too intense to ignore. He stifled another moan.

"Liz," he gasped, tangling his fingers in her hair.

Her wide red lips slid up and down his shaft. His body clenched, his cock drained by her eager ministrations.

"Oh, honey," he moaned.

"Spice," she corrected and then pulled him to his feet.

Sean didn't remember the trip to the bedroom, because he was too busy kissing her, tasting his pleasure on her lips. Her silk-wrapped hand was back around his cock. He closed the door and locked it.

"Now, you're mine," he said, backing her onto the bed. Her hand pumped him back into hardness. He held the back of her head while he ravaged her neck with sucking bites.

"Please," Liz begged.

"Please what?" Sean growled in her ear.

"I need you."

He flipped her on her stomach, pushing the kimono up her back. Her beautiful ass tempted him, and he darted down for a quick taste.

She screeched into the pillow.

"Later," he promised with one last lick at her tight entrance. "Are you ready for me?"

He tested her wetness and became distracted by the glistening pearl between her legs. He stroked it until she was gasping into the pillow. Sean couldn't wait any longer.

He plunged into her heat and rammed himself back and forth. Guiding her hips, he slammed hard and fast, feeling her tight grip milk him.

"Yes," Liz screamed, muffling the sound as best as she could.

He took her with every longing, every dirty thought he ever had. When the room was spinning for him, he held himself still deep inside her and admired how she looked. Her pretty face was tilted to the side, jaw slack with pleasure. Her pussy clenched and unclenched around him like her silk-covered hand.

"Where's the lube?" he asked.

She pointed to the bedside table.

"Get it," Sean ordered and moved with her so when his cock slid out, he thrust back in.

She tossed him a bottle of coconut oil.

He positioned himself behind her again and now took his time drawing in and out of her. Liz sighed, her body relaxed and pliable. The sound of the wetness coating him as he fucked her was driving him near the edge. He pushed deep as he could and held her there.

She moaned. "Don't stop." Then he poured the coconut oil over her ass, making sure some got into her sweet little hole.

Liz clamped down hard-on his cock and he almost went off right there. Sean kneaded her ass cheeks, gave them a little smack just to see them jiggle.

Her hips rotated slow little circles around his cock.

"Yeah," he moaned, lost in the sensation.

His finger circled her ass on the outside, just the rim.

"Sean," she cried out. "I can take it. I was a DP Queen."

"Not for a while you haven't. Slow, remember?"

"You're making me crazy," Liz panted.

"Good."

He resumed fucking her, but his balls were ready to burst—even after the world class blow job she gave him. He wanted to feel her shake apart around him. Deep again, he stopped. But her hips kept going. Damn, this was going to have to be quick.

Making sure his finger was coated thick with the coconut oil, he dipped the tip of it inside her hole and made small circles inside the opening. Liz's hips were forcing up and down his shaft and her movements hit just right and his finger was inside her.

"Yes," she moved faster. Slippery, he tried to keep up. She took his finger so well, he tried for two. It was tight, but the oil eased the way. He let her set the pace. He came almost immediately, but grabbed her shoulder so he could stay inside her as long as it took. Shudders shook his entire body as he came. Her sweet pussy took it all, clamping down in a hard grip.

"Liz!" he cried, his vision narrowing. He was pretty sure his head just exploded. Sean's heart was threatening to beat out of his chest. This was the most erotic moment of his life. Liz would forever be his fantasy.

She was wild, taking her pleasure. She was moaning his name over and over again, as lost in the erotic play of his body in hers as he was. One final squeeze, and Liz screamed, her cries barely muffled by the pillow. He eased away and flopped next to her, hugging her close. He could feel her breasts through the kimono, firm and sexy. Kissing the top of her head, Sean wished this moment could last forever. But he was going to tell her everything and hoped to God she didn't hate him for it.

So this is heaven, Liz thought as she splayed across Sean's body. He had pulled the kimono down so she wasn't cold and was rubbing circles over her back. If he kept this up, she'd be asleep and drooling on him. Every inch of her felt loved and pleasured. Satisfaction hummed through her entire body.

She leaned up to nibble on his ear. "I want to do it again." Then she giggled when he pulled her completely on top of him.

"If there was anyone who could get me hard for a third time tonight, it's you."

They kissed again, for what seemed like hours. Her leg tossed over his, she felt him harden after a while.

"I need to tell you something," Sean said. His face buried in her neck. She was going to have bruises from his love bites there tomorrow, but that's what turtlenecks were for.

She sighed. "Actually, I should go first. I have a problem."

With on last tug on her neck, he propped himself up on his elbow. "Let me help you with the problem." He traced her cheekbone down to her lips.

Liz's eyes closed. He was trouble. She was falling for him. And her life was becoming a train wreck. "I had a visitor today." She said and then told him the whole story and who they thought the likely candidates were.

"I want you to call me as soon as you get another one." Sean's face darkened, and she could feel the rage coming off him.

"You think I'm going to get another one? That this wasn't a joke?" Liz knew in her heart of hearts that was probably the case, but she had held out hope.

"I know there is. This joker is playing a game. Whether it's your ex or that reporter or something more sinister, you need to be on your guard at all time. Mischief Night and Halloween are coming up. You and Jonathan are going to be with me on those nights. I don't want you alone here. I can stay here, if you want, or you can come to my place."

"What about your roommates?"

"Never mind about that. I'm worried for you. Wednesday, you're getting a self-defense lesson, too."

"Do you think we're really in danger?"

"I don't know. But we're going to go about it as if this person is a crazy stalker. The minute it even hints at being dangerous, I want you to go to the police."

Liz nodded. "I hope it doesn't come to that."

"Me too, darlin', me too."

She shivered. Oh, she had missed that little brogue. Reaching down, she guided him back inside her. Their lovemaking was slow. She stared into his eyes the entire time. When she came, she bit his shoulder, but he didn't seem to mind. He came, whispering all the dirty things he was going to do to her, in that lilting Irish accent.

When she recovered, she kissed the bite mark on his shoulder. "What were you going to tell me?"

"It can wait," he said. "Until you and Jonathan are safe."

Chapter Twelve

Sean was happy that no DVDs or any other presents found their way to Liz's door since that stunning night of amazing sex. All day on Monday, he walked around with a dopey grin on his face. It only started to fade last night, but the fact that he was seeing her today was enough to start him smiling again. His only regret was he couldn't meet Jonathan without still carrying his secrets. But he couldn't risk her shutting him out when she might need his protection. He failed Mary Katherine. He wasn't going to fail Liz.

Of course, she was going to figure it out sooner or later. But hopefully, her stalker or whoever it was would be long gone by then. If Sean caught him, he'd beat the son of a bitch into hamburger meat.

"Morning, Gladys," he said.

"Sean, thanks for coming in early to see Jackie Starke."

"Not a problem. Send her in when she gets here, would you?"

"I put her file on your desk. She's had a few more altercations in school."

Sean made a face. "Are we sure she's taking her meds?"

"That's where you come in."

"I'm on it." He gave her a salute and then made a beeline to the coffeemaker. Sean wasn't comfortable yet with the dosages. He was glad Dr. Strauss and Gladys were supervising his decisions. He still had a few thousand hours to go before he could apply for his therapist license, and he was glad he could learn hands-on. He brought her over a cup before going into his office.

"Bless you," Gladys said, her hand over the mouthpiece of the phone.

Sean needed the coffee. His schedule was going to kill him. He resisted the urge to lay his forehead down on his desk. Days like this, he thought, *fuck it*. Maybe he should ditch it all and become a stripper and a boxer. He'd quit the university job. Liz would never have to know he was a doctoral candidate. He'd let McManus mold him into the fighter he thought Sean could be and, when money got tight, he could go back to Club 69.

It was a nice fantasy. One he wondered if Mary Katherine actually acted on. When her audition for the Rockettes came back with a "don't call us, we'll call you," she was devastated. The first time he ever heard her cry was on the phone when she got the rejection letter. Their mother told her to come back home. She could teach dancing or go back to school and get a business degree. But she stayed in Manhattan. If faced with stripping or living with his parents on the island, he'd pick stripping, too.

But why the drugs?

Sugar and Spice got out of the business and Sarah and Liz were the most normal women he knew—and sexy as hell. Mary Katherine was strong, as strong as they were. If they didn't numb with alcohol or drugs, she wouldn't have either. So maybe it wasn't about being numb.

This was going to drive him crazy. Maybe he should go to one of the psychics and ask them to channel Mary Katherine. "Hi Squirt," she'd say, and he'd probably start bawling. He went back for his second cup of coffee before tackling his paperwork.

Gladys shrugged at him as he went by, indicating she didn't know where Jackie was. If she was with her mother, she would have been here by now. Chances were she was at her father's house this week. He was always a half hour late, if he even bothered to bring her. His daughter wasn't crazy, blah blah blah. She doesn't need therapy. Shit, after a half hour talking with him, Sean needed therapy. He couldn't imagine living with the tool every other week.

He was searching for foundations that would donate a couple of laptops to the clinic when he came across the website for the Canning Foundation. They had hooked up McManus for all the youth boxing equipment. Then it hit him, who Cole really was. Cole Canning, Executive Director of the Canning Foundation. Normally, they worked with children of cancer patients and granted them special trips and experiences, but they were also donating to local youth programs.

He picked up his cell and called the number on the website. He expected and got Cole's answering machine. "Hey, it's Sean O'Malley. We had dinner on Saturday. I'm an idiot, I just realized I should have thanked you personally for your foundation's grant to my gym. That's the gym that McManus owns. The kids really like it and the equipment is put to good use. They have after-school programs every day, and I'm there on Monday, Wednesday, and Friday. If you're available, stop by and I'll give you a tour and we can go a few rounds. Thanks again."

Sean hit up their online form and put in a proposal for six new or used laptops to be used in occupational therapy. He liked Gladys's idea to grab the kids who wanted to work with computers instead of in the gym.

The knock on his door had him standing automatically, ready to shake Jackie's hand, but Sabrina sauntered in. Gladys rolled her eyes before leaving them alone. At least this time Sabrina was sober.

"Have you had a chance to think about my offer?" Sabrina said. She wore a tight mini dress with a big V cut out at the chest and knee-length black boots. It wasn't doing anything for him.

He had it bad for Liz.

"I don't think it's for me," Sean said. "Want a soda?"

"Sure." Sabrina eased into the seat and deliberately rubbed her leg against his when he handed her the can.

Sean went back behind his desk. "I'm not sure how long I can spend with you today. I've got a full schedule. But I'm glad you came back. I'm sorry if I said things you didn't want to hear."

"I'm not a doper," she said. "I just wanted to set the record straight. I like to have a good time. I smoke a little J. Sometimes I pop a few pills. But it's not an addiction."

"Okay," Sean said. "I stand corrected." He remembered what Gladys had advised: just sit back and let it come on out.

"Desiree wasn't an addict either." Sabrina was fierce when she wasn't stoned. She held his gaze until he acknowledged her words.

Sean nodded, his throat tight.

"I don't think she committed suicide," she frowned. "That's what the buzz was all over the set. It wasn't foul play either." Sabrina played with the tab on her can. "Everybody loved her. I think it was just one big accident. But I'm not sure." She shook her head, her blonde hair shining in the dull florescent lights. He noticed her makeup was more subtle this time, but her body language was aggressive. Sabrina leaned forward so her breasts were more noticeable. She licked her lips as a nervous gesture, but she looked at him under her eyelashes to see if he was watching.

"Tell me about the dopers." Sean held on to his coffee like a lifeline. He didn't know what her deal was, if this was her way of flirting or if this is how she related to all men, but he wasn't interested and never would be. She simply wasn't his type. His type was a sensual brunette who made his cock hard just by talking.

"I'm pretty sure I don't have to tell you what they're like. You're the one with the degrees and shit in this. But I will tell you the stereotype doesn't exist. Half-baked girls don't fuck on camera unless they want to. It's not like they're toking up to get through the pain of the day or any of that bullshit. Are there girls like that? Sure. Do directors cast them? No. Who wants to deal with all that emo drama?"

Sabrina finished her soda and tossed the can into the trash. Standing up, she prowled around the room, looking at his diplomas, eyeing the cabinets.

"So if they're not getting work with the big studios, how do they pay rent?" Sean swiveled his chair to make sure he kept her in full sight. He wouldn't put it past her to swipe something—not that there was anything she could pawn within reach.

"Some go into prostitution." Sabrina ran her hand down her front and tipped up her skirt at him.

Sean's lips tightened.

"Some start selling as well as using."

He shook his head.

"Some get the fuck out of the business." She perched her hip on his desk and emphasized the word *fuck*.

"What would you do, if the offers started drying up?" He moved out of her reach when she tried to touch her leg to his again.

Sabrina laughed. "Move to LA. Suck my way across country and then set up shop. I may still do that anyway." She looked off into the distance and seemed to get lost in her thoughts.

"Was Mary—Desiree going to California?"

Sabrina blinked, as though she forgot where she was. She ran a hand through her hair. "We talked about it. But she liked it here too much. Her family meant a lot to her. I meant it before when I said she wouldn't want you to blame yourself. Look," she hopped off the desk and walked toward the door. "I think you'd learn a lot if you came to the audition," she said over her shoulder. "You'd understand the process a little better. Think of it as firsthand research or something."

"Primary source," Sean said, smiling. "I'll think about it."

She turned and struck a dramatic pose in the doorway. "I know it's out of your comfort zone. But that's kind of the point, isn't it?"

His phone rang.

"I should take this," he said.

"I'll see you Thursday." She blew him a kiss.

"O'Malley," Sean said into the phone, resisting the urge to roll his eyes.

"Sean, it's Cole. I got your message."

"Damn, that was quick," Sean adjusted the phone on his shoulder so he could type some notes into his calendar at the same time. "Thanks again. The equipment you donated to the gym does a lot of good for those kids."

"No problem. I was looking to see if you're free next Wednesday for that tour?"

Sean checked his calendar. "How does 4:30 sound?"

"Perfect. I'll see you then."

After they hung up, Sean realized his name was all over the clinic's grant proposal and he had left Cole his office number instead of his cell phone number. He never told Liz he worked here. He didn't want Gladys or Dr. Jenkins unknowingly revealing his true academic status. Sean would just have to hope Cole wouldn't mention it to Liz. This was getting complicated. Tangled webs and all that. It was getting harder to keep his lies straight.

"So is your friend nice?" Jonathan asked. "Have Sarah, and Peter, and Honey met him?"

Liz hooked her arm around him in the back of the taxi. "Cole and Sarah have met him. They think he's pretty cool."

"Don't say cool."

"Why?"

"Because cool is for kids. You should say grown-up words." Jonathan rolled his eyes at her.

"Okay, smart boy, what's a grown up word for cooooooool?" Liz drew out the word and was rewarded with an exasperated sigh.

"Laudable."

"Laudable?" Liz laughed. "All right. Yes, they think he's laudable. Where did you hear that from?"

"It was one of my daily words on the calendar you gave me."

Liz shook her head; he was too smart for her. She hoped Jonathan liked Sean. They got out at the gym and went inside. A class of kids about Jonathan's age was just coming in the door. Jonathan stepped away, as though he didn't want to be associated with her, and walked in after them. He darted a glance over his shoulder to make sure she followed, though.

The kids knew where to go and headed back to the locker room area. Liz saw a couple of fighters in the ring going at it and McManus yelling pointers. She caught up to Jonathan and, since he was already in his exercise clothes, she walked him to the area that Sean had shown her.

He was there, stretching out on the mat. But he got up to his feet in one lithe movement when he saw them come in.

"Glad you could make it." He kissed her on the cheek and held out his hand to Jonathan. "I'm Sean O'Malley. You must be Jonathan. Your mom told me all about you."

"What did she say?" Jonathan narrowed his eyes at her.

"She said you liked Transformers and Legos."

Jonathan looked over his shoulder and lowered his voice. "That's kids' stuff. I like it, though."

"Me too," Sean whispered back. "I won't tell if you won't. Fist bump?"

Jonathan bumped fists with him.

"So do you want to watch for a bit or get right into the class? We're going to go over some very basic stuff."

"What kind of stuff?" Liz asked.

"No sparring," he assured her.

"Aw," Jonathan moaned.

"You have to learn how to hit and how to be hit before you can get into the ring. Safety, first."

"You sound like my mom," he groaned.

"Good." Sean winked at Liz. "I see you're dressed for some exercise, too. We can work on some moves when I pair up the kids."

A smile tickled her lips. There were a lot of moves she'd like to try on him.

He returned the smile as if he knew what she was thinking.

Their intimate moment was broken by the fifteen or so kids coming in. They all wore the same red shirt and red gym shorts. Sean lined them up in three rows and had them do arm and leg stretches. After a few jumping jacks, he handed out the jump ropes.

Liz was content to watch. She didn't think she'd be half as graceful as he was. He started them off slow and then faster. The only sounds in the gym were the whizzing of the ropes and the pounding feet on the mat.

"Good," he said. "Let's suit up and do some drills." Sean handed out helmets and gloves. "Get a partner to help you with your gloves."

He walked over to where Liz was sitting down.

"Hey, beautiful."

She could feel herself blushing. To cover her embarrassment, she said, "Those gloves are bigger than he is." Liz kept her voice down so Jonathan wouldn't notice her talking about him. "Are you sure the headgear is protective enough?"

"The gloves are regulation sixteen ounces. The headgear is professional grade. It's like the one I use, only smaller. The only thing different about this gear is we skip the mouthguards with the beginner class because they're not facing off against each other. Don't worry, sweetheart. He's going to be fine."

He turned back to the class and clapped for their attention. "Line up on the vertical yellow lines. Yellow lines only please. Okay, we're going to stand like boxers. Any lefties in class?" He looked around. A few kids raised their hands. "Do everything opposite of what I tell you. I'll demonstrate both lefty and righty stances."

Sean got into his stance. Liz felt a trill of awareness drift over her. He looked like a tiger about to pounce.

"Straddle the line. Righties step forward and put your left toe on the line. Put the heel of your back foot on the line. Feet diagonal. Shoulder width. Lefties, just the opposite. Like this." He showed them. "Stay loose. Don't be so stiff. Bend your knees a bit. Raise your back heel. You want your weight evenly distributed. This should start to feel natural. Gloves up. Elbows down. You're protecting your face with your gloves and your ribs with your elbows. Got it?"

Sean reversed his pose. He went to every child and corrected stances and how they were holding their gloves. Jonathan was spot on. Pride warred with trepidation.

"Look over your gloves, drop your chin. Protect your head with your gloves. Righties, put your right hand in back by your chin. Left hand in front. Lefties copy me. Excellent. I see a bunch of you holding your breath. Breathe. Let's try some footwork drills. Step and drag. Step and drag."

Sean had them do that up and down the gym.

"Now let's work on pivoting."

He had them do a few more techniques and the class followed along diligently. He was a good teacher. Sean had a way with the children. They looked up to him. Although, he lost them a few times when he got too technical with some of the descriptions.

"Let's practice punching."

"Yes," Jonathan said, along with a few other students.

"Spread out." Sean waved his hands. "No contact. Watch me first."

He demonstrated the different types of punches: jab, right cross, left hook, overhand right, left uppercut, right uppercut, body . . . He started to lose her when he went into combos.

"Now you guys. Jab. Keep going."

Sean again walked around. They went over each punch several times. Sean corrected their stances, their footwork. He was patient and supportive. When he took time with Jonathan to correct him, Liz had to blink back tears. Sarah's Cole showed her what Jonathan had been missing. The guy presence. Jonathan deserved someone like Sean in his life. Liz inhaled sharply when she realized the truth: so did she.

The lesson wound down shortly after a flurry of combinations that looked like a windmill to her. Sean had them put away the equipment and promised them if they did it neatly, he'd let them watch the sparring matches in the other side of the gym until their rides came.

Sean sat down next to her. "What did you think?"

"You were great. Jonathan is enthralled. Thank you."

"He's welcome any time." Sean nudged her with his shoulder. "I missed you."

"You could have called." Liz hid a smile. Just because she was head over heels for him didn't mean she was going to make it easy on him.

"I was dead on my feet. The phone works both ways."

"I had to finish up on the raffle tickets and the posters for the Halloween dance next Friday. Jonathan's school is doing a fundraiser," she explained. "I was volunteered."

"Are you going to go to the dance?"

"I promised Jonathan we'd do some trick or treating, but, yeah, we're going to end up at the dance afterward."

"Want company?"

"You're going to have to dress in costume," she warned.

"What are you guys going as?"

"I'm going to be Cinderella and he's going as the Red Power Ranger."

"I'll be your prince," Sean whispered in her ear.

"Get out." She pushed him.

"How hard can a prince costume be?"

"Are you serious?" Maybe he really was Mr. Perfect after all. She put her hand on his leg and lightly tickled her fingers up his thigh. "I'd make it worth your while."

"I'm not up on *Cinderella*," he admitted. "My sister made me watch it a long time ago. Is he a tights-wearing prince?"

"We can watch it tonight," Jonathan said. Liz jumped guiltily as if he'd caught her necking in the corner with her boyfriend. "It's my mom's favorite movie. She's seen it a bazillion times. She always cries when Cinderelly sings 'A Dream is a Wish Your Heart Makes.'"

Sean hooked an arm around her shoulders and brought her in for a kiss on the temple. "Sounds like we're getting the pizza to go. Let me get the kids settled in watching the matches so I can take a shower and then we can get out of here."

"Can I watch the matches, too?" Jonathan asked.

"Sure," Liz said, crinkling her nose. "After your shower."

Chapter Thirteen

We never got around to talking about self-defense," Sean said as she finished tucking Jonathan into bed.

"I'm too content to think about fighting." Liz closed the door on her son's room and joined Sean on the couch, straddling his legs. He immediately cupped her ass, bringing her closer.

Toying with the hair on the back of his neck, she waited for him to kiss her. It had been the best night she had in a long time. Jonathan had come out of the showers like a damp puppy, all wiggles and excitement. Sean explained who each of the fighters were in the ring and what their strong points and weak points were. On the way to the pizza place, Jonathan remembered he had homework. Liz put her foot down and said they'd have to get delivery. She had expected tears or a tantrum, but Jonathan agreed—as long as Sean helped him out with the math worksheets.

Sean was staring at her with an intensity that turned her on. Shifting, she opened her knees so his hardness rested between her thighs. Tingles warmed her body. He slipped his hands inside her yoga pants.

"Take off your shirt," Sean asked, holding her tight against him when she would have pulled away. "You can leave your bra on."

"Can I?" she said, tartly. "Jonathan isn't asleep yet."

"That's why my cock isn't inside you," he whispered in her ear.

She held on to his shoulders and rocked against him. He squeezed her ass and tugged on her earlobe with a warning bite. Liz melted. She had no defenses against the erotic surge he caused in her. "This is getting serious for me."

"For me too," he said. "You're incredible. Jonathan's incredible. I want to be a part of your life."

Joyous little sparks lit up inside her. If explaining ten frames to Jonathan and her so they both actually got it, from the theory to the practice, didn't scare him off, she had been convinced that her sniffling into a tissue during *Cinderella* would have.

"I have to tell you a few things," he said. "About my sister and some of the choices I've made since she died."

Liz stroked his hair, reveling in the lush thickness of it. She wanted to feel it between her thighs. Kissing his forehead, she squirmed closer to him.

"I know this isn't easy for you," she said.

"My sister was a porn actress."

Liz sat back so she could look at him. "A famous one? Would I know her?"

He shook his head. "I don't think so. She worked in New York." Sean sighed. "We grew up on the south shore of Long Island. All she ever wanted to be was a New York City Rockette. She was a majorette in the band. Mary Katherine practiced her high kicks every chance she got—with whoever was around. I'm sure there are some pictures of me and her, her arm slung around my shoulders practicing her kick line."

The desire banked to a low simmer of intimacy that nearly took her breath away. She pulled her T-shirt over her head. Her sports bra held in her reconstructive breasts and Liz thought she still looked pretty normal from this angle. His quick intake of breath turned her shy gaze back to him.

"I don't want to interrupt your story. But you're baring your soul right now, I can tell. The least I can do is bare my chest. I've got scars," she warned, tracing where they were over her bra.

He traced where she indicated with a feathery touch. She couldn't feel it in the traditional manner, but the tender concern on his face quickened her breath.

"Thank you," he said, hugging her close. His face buried in her cleavage, Liz fought panic. But it faded, once she realized he wasn't going to try for more and was satisfied with just holding her. She cuddled him close and enjoyed his nearness. He kissed her chest and up to her neck, nuzzling her cheek and ear. "You are so beautiful."

"I don't feel it."

He kissed her cheek. "You will. I promise. I need to tell you about Mary Katherine, though. I've waited too long to do this."

"You said she died of a drug overdose," Liz said, stroking his cheek.

"It was a big shock. I identified the body. I didn't want to inflict that on my parents. We all thought it was a big mistake. But there she was. I wish things had been different and that she would have confided in me."

"Did you know she was doing the adult films?"

Sean circled his hands over her back. She rested her cheek against his. It seemed to soothe him. "No. None of us did. We figured she was waitressing or doing office work while she interviewed. She started out as a stripper, but then got into the films. My parents still don't know. They think someone slipped her the drugs and she accidentally took them."

"What do you think?"

"I think it wasn't the first time she used the hand-blown glass pipe that was in her personal effects. You want to know the fuck of it, Liz?"

Liz raised her head and nodded. "Tell me."

"It was the prettiest damn thing I've ever seen. It had facets and colors like a prism. It was just the type of thing she would hang in her window, except of course it had drugs in it." He let out a large sigh.

"Do you think she turned to drugs out of depression or guilt or something related to porn?"

"You're very insightful. NYU is lucky to have you as a student." He kissed her lips, and a spark arced though them both.

"Next semester anyways," she blushed. "I've got it all worked out. Sarah is going to pick up Jonathan on Mondays so I can be available— even if they don't need me. That way I can work on my homework and not have to worry about rushing back. Want to be my study partner?" She batted her eyes at him.

"We'd never get any work done." He kissed her again.

"We would." She darted her tongue against his. "After."

The kissing was unavoidable. She attacked him with greedy kisses, easing up only when she pulled his sweater over his head.

"Should we take this into the bedroom?" he said.

"Not just yet," Liz rubbed his shoulders. "You're holding something back, I can feel it."

"Take off your bra."

Liz was surprised that she was tempted. She wanted him to see her. Wanted him to still want her after seeing the lifeless lumps. "They're not pretty," she said in a small voice. "They don't look like breasts. In addition to the scars, I don't have nipples. There aren't any nerve endings so I can't feel a kiss or your tongue. They're useless really."

"I think they're sexy," he said.

"That's because they're covered," she joked and shuddered when he held them in his hands.

"You feel that," Sean said.

"Not like . . ." Words failed her. It wasn't a sexual feeling, yet him touching her like she was normal—the idea that if she had her D-cups back, he'd be paying attention to them like this—shook her. Liz saw him rub his thumb over where her nipples should have been, and it made her wet. He squeezed her breasts and hummed his appreciation.

"Nice," he said.

For the first time since the surgery, she felt sexy and normal. She didn't want the feeling to end. He slipped the straps of her bra down her shoulders. The first of her scars were showing.

"Sean," Liz whispered. If he recoiled or turned away, she would die.

His tongue traced the scar. She started to shiver.

"God," she gritted out, pulling on his hair to bring him closer. Grinding on his hard cock, she knew she was soaking her pants and his. "Please." Her head dipped back when he traced the other scar. "You can't."

He kissed the top of each breast and leaned back against the couch.

"Too much. Not tonight." Liz broke away. "You're not mad?"

Sean shook his head. "I want you too much. I can wait."

Rotating her hips, Liz licked her lips. "I want this," she ground down on his hard bulge. "In my mouth, my pussy, and my ass."

"You're going to make me come in my pants," he chided. "And I still haven't told you what I need to."

"I keep interrupting you."

"I don't mind. I'd put off this conversation if I could." His hands were in the back of her pants, spreading her cheeks.

"Baby steps," she told him and bit his neck.

"What?" he grunted, thrusting up into her.

"It's what I tell myself when I get overwhelmed," Liz licked the long column of his throat. "Rome wasn't built in a day, that sort of thing." She nibbled on his jaw line. "As long as you start something, it's forward motion."

He tickled her ass, rubbing the outside of her hole.

"Oh," she cried. "What was I saying?"

"You were saying, 'Fuck me hard, Sean,'" he prompted.

Her lips hovered over his. "Not yet. Let's see. You're not in a race. You'll get there eventually. I'm not going anywhere." She pressed a kiss on his nose. "Except the bedroom."

Wiggling off him, she dropped her pants, panties and all, and crooked her finger at him. "Talk after," she said.

When he stood, Liz launched herself at him, wrapping her legs around his waist. For a moment, he staggered and she thought they were going to fall back on the couch. But Sean steadied himself and walked with her to the bedroom, his mouth never leaving hers.

Kicking the door closed, Sean whirled, pressing her back to the door. Still kissing her, he fumbled his belt and pants while her legs tightened on his chest. Guiding his cock into her, Sean's first thrust rattled the door frame.

"Shh," she warned, as they both listened. But there wasn't any stirring from the other room.

He fucked her slow, his hands supporting her thighs. He filled her and then pulled all the way out to the tip, then repeated the movement until she thought she'd go mad. She wanted more. She wanted it hard and fast. She wanted him to pound her through the door. Liz couldn't stop kissing him, even when her orgasm clenched her pussy around him. Sean groaned in pleasure. Her legs trembled and went weak. Carrying her over to the bed, he placed her gently on her back. Then Sean lifted her legs and pinned them back behind her ears.

"Now," he grunted. "I'm not holding back."

Liz didn't want him to. His fast, deep thrusts hit her erogenous zones. His eyes were dark and feral. She felt ravaged, taken, and thoroughly pleasured. He came after burying himself to the hilt. Sean's breathing was ragged, his eyes unfocused. Liz took advantage of that moment, gripping him still, to reach over to the bedside table and open the drawer.

"Take this," she said, handing him a slim vibrator.

"Where do you want this?" he asked, taking the coconut oil from her and lubing it up.

"Where do you think?"

Sean grunted. "I don't think it's going to work at this angle."

"Ease out for a second," Liz murmured. "Kneel on the bed."

Sean followed her orders and gasped when she crawled over to take him in his mouth. She could taste her own juices on him and the tang of his release. Moaning, Liz took all of him in her mouth and felt him start to get hard again.

He didn't need further instructions. Liz felt him spread her ass checks and drizzle the oil in between them. His fingers were gentle, even as his body was tensing from the hard sucks she was giving his cock. When he penetrated her with the dildo, Liz moaned. Sean gripped her ass with one hand and thrust the little dildo in and out. Her head bobbed up and down, sliding her tongue over his hardness. He stopped with the dildo, pushing it in so it held there.

"Get on your back," Sean commanded.

Reluctantly, Liz let his cock out of her mouth. She obeyed him and, as he moved to loom over her, she turned to take him in her mouth again.

"Yeah, just like that. Suck my cock."

He tapped the dildo to make sure it was staying in place. Then he pushed one finger inside her pussy. Then two. The oil flowing, he guided a third into her. Liz started to shake. He fucked her with his fingers, in and out, the rhythm matching with her sucking on his cock.

Liz swallowed as Sean came down her throat in a thick rush. Moaning, as his fingers plucked her clit, Liz allowed him to slip out of her mouth. Then he moved into a position where he could replace the fingers in her pussy with his tongue.

"Sean," she gasped, so close to her own orgasm that she was nearly incoherent.

"I want you to come," he growled, licking her throbbing clit.

Her hips rose to take more of him and, while his greedy tongue probed her, she shook with release. Kissing her pussy up to her stomach, Sean clutched her to him. "I will never get tired of making you come."

Liz was too breathless to speak. Her body twitched with sensations as he stroked her back. The dildo in her backside was pure decadent sensation.

Take me. Take all of me.

She held him close.

Never let me go.

Chapter Fourteen

Sean couldn't believe he was doing this. He'd left Liz's apartment when Sarah and little Christopher showed up to walk Jonathan to school. The look on Sarah's face had been priceless. Liz had managed a smug, serene smile for her friend, but he was guessing as soon as Jonathan was in class, the two of them would be talking.

He'd planned on grabbing breakfast on campus before his class. But instead, he took a train downtown. Talking about Mary Katherine—even though he didn't get a chance to tell Liz everything—freed something inside him. Sean was going to take this to the very end—put some real data through his algorithms and see if the porn industry did sprout drug abusers more than another profession.

So that's how he found himself on the elevator on a Thursday morning, going to a porn audition instead of teaching his Intro to Social Work course. He owed Mike a six pack of Killians and a couple of Ruebens for taking his classes today. The hotel was a generic business center, with conference rooms on every floor. He was heading to the bridal suite. The irony almost made him smile.

He tried to picture Mary Katherine taking this same route. What would she be feeling? The thought that she had been scared made him want to beat something. He had searched through all her things, but he wasn't able to figure out if she had been in trouble or had been blackmailed into it.

The autopsy showed she had taken a lethal amount of crystallized meth, or ice. It had caused a heart attack. They had an open casket funeral for her. God, he hated those things. The deceased always looked like spent balloons. Except Mary Katherine. She looked like she was sleeping. She didn't have any signs of the scarring or abrasions of a typical meth addict. They didn't rule it a suicide—thank God. Otherwise they would've buried his mother, too. Mary Katherine's purse had been on her shoulder. Her apartment keys were in her hand. She was dressed up to go somewhere nice. They found her facedown on her bedroom floor.

It was a small comfort that she didn't suffer.

The police ruled out foul play. The pipe had only her finger and lip prints on it and the drug hadn't been tampered with. It just had been too much for her body to handle.

Mary Katherine had been a talented dancer and a health nut. She would hide their father's cigarettes and nag at him to quit until an asthma attack made the decision for him. She demanded organic and free-range food to the point that their mother told her if she wanted that high-priced stuff, she could get a damn job and buy it herself. So she did. And converted their mother to buying organic after a few taste tests.

The elevator stopped, jostling him out of his thoughts as it let him off on the penthouse floor. At his knock, the door opened and a rotund man jawing on an unlit cigar waved him in.

"You must be Sabrina's friend. Sam?"

"Sean," he said.

"Good to meetcha. I'm Allen. I'm going to be the director of this flick."

Sean wasn't sure if he was supposed to shake his hand, but Allen turned and walked further into the room. The suite was set up as a film shoot. There were cameras on tripods, screens, and mirrors. A few guys sat in the kitchen, drinking coffee. The cameramen were setting up in the large bedroom area. Sean saw a king-sized bed.

"Can I get you something to eat or drink?"

"I'm good," Sean said. The thought of anything in his stomach right now was not a good idea. None of this was. "I'm actually here as an observer."

"Uh huh," Allen said. "One of those, huh? Look, either get in the bathroom and take off your clothes or get the hell out." He indicated the door with his head.

Sean looked around. There were only guys here. It was just like the locker room at the gym, only weirder. "I have to take my clothes off to audition?"

"What do you think you're auditioning with, your mind?"

There was that. Well, he had wanted the full experience, and this was part of it. Would Mary Katherine have stripped and come out of the bathroom naked and proud? Would she have huddled against the sink and taken a few pills to get up her courage. Sean frowned. Of either image, the first one was more like his sister than the second. Mary Katherine didn't cower from anything. Not their father in his drunken rages, not their mother with her wooden spoon. She would have stripped and then said, "Now what?"

If he wanted to get a grasp on what her last few days were like, he had to do it.

"Fine," Sean said and closed the bathroom door behind him.

He wanted to text Liz. But he didn't want her tainted by this. What on Earth would she say if she knew he was here? She'd try to talk him out of it, or worse, she and Sarah would laugh about it. Sean switched off his phone and took his time taking off his clothes. Unlike stripping, there was nothing powerful or erotic in shedding them in a hotel bathroom while a crew of men talked sports outside. When he couldn't stall any longer, he came out of the bathroom with his clothes positioned in front of his junk.

"Get in the bedroom," Allen said. "We want to see how the camera paints you."

What the fuck did that mean?

But when he got into the bedroom, he saw Sabrina was on that big bed. She was naked and sprawled out. Sean averted his eyes. "What the hell are you doing here?"

"I'm your sex partner for today," she said, giggling.

He risked a look at her eyes. High. Shit. Not that he was going to fuck her sober or wasted, on camera or off. The only woman he wanted was right now cackling with her best friend over Starbucks and a scone.

"Drop your clothes, Sam. No need to be shy."

"It's Sean," he said to the director. While he was distracted, Sabrina lunged for him and managed to snatch his clothes out of his grip.

"Gotcha," she giggled.

He refused to be embarrassed. He didn't have anything that any other man didn't have. Sean wasn't an exhibitionist, but he wasn't a prude.

"It'll do," Allen said, nodding. "Get in the bed. The first scene is a sixty-nine. You want me to call in a fluffer?"

"I'll do it," Sabrina said and reached for his cock.

Sean danced back like he was in the ring. "The hell you will. Look, I made a mistake here. I'm not fucking you."

"No one said anything about fucking right now. Start with eating her pussy and we'll go from there. All right?" Allen gestured to the cameraman.

"No."

"Action."

"Come here, handsome," Sabrina said, massaging her hands over her breasts.

"You can suck her tits first if you want," Allen said, helpfully.

"What the fuck is going on here?" a stocky man, fully dressed, stormed into the bedroom. He wasn't looking too happy.

"Who the fuck are you?" Allen said. "This isn't a gang bang."

"Oh, that's just my boyfriend, Brian." Sabrina laughed. "He's a cameraman. I called him to see if he wanted to watch."

"This isn't what it looks like," Sean said, wishing he wasn't naked. He grabbed his pants and underwear.

Brian ignored him and held out his hand. "Come with me, Sabrina. This isn't a safe operation. I've heard bad things about this company."

"Hey," Allen said. "Fuck you. Stay away from my talent."

"I'm leaving here with my girlfriend or I'm telling the hotel manager just what's happening in the bridal suite. Got that, asshole?" Brian got in Allen's face.

"I don't want any trouble." Allen put up placating hands. "But this is all consensual."

"I'm not consenting," Sean said, buttoning his pants and looking around for his socks and shoes.

"I'm safe," Sabrina said, plucking at the sheets. She looked up at Brian with big eyes. Her pupils were almost completely dilated.

Didn't anyone see that? Or care?

"A real production company does background checks and confirms STD tests. You don't know what this guy has." Brian waved his hand at Sean.

Before Sean could open his mouth to argue that he wasn't actually going to go through with the scene, Sabrina cut him off. "He's clean, Brian. He's Desiree's brother. The one that was going to be a doctor."

Brian cut him a look.

"You knew my sister?" Sean said, pulling on his socks and shoes. Now, if he could only find his shirt.

Great. It's on the pillow.

"His background checks out." Sabrina continued as if he hadn't spoken. "He works with at-risk kids in Queens and teaches at NYU. He's a first-timer."

"What the hell are you doing here?" Brian asked him.

Sean plucked his shirt off the bed before Sabrina could grab it again. "It's complicated," he said.

And I'm a big idiot.

"He wants to see what drove his sister to overdose." Sabrina lay back on the pillows and pouted.

"And none of you lifted a finger to stop her," Sean accused.

"I didn't know it was that bad until it was too late," Sabrina said.

"The drugs had nothing to do with this." Brian waved his hand around the hotel room. "I knew Desiree. She didn't have a problem with fucking on camera. In fact, she loved it. She was talking about doing webcasts from her bedroom to cut out the middle man." Sean resisted the urge to flatten the prick. "She did women, men, both. It didn't matter. She got top dollar to do anal and if she moved to LA, she would have been as big as Sugar or Spice."

Sean flinched. As if he didn't already feel like the world's biggest asshole, now he had to realize that his sister had a healthy sex life, and that, as a porn actress, she was on par with his girlfriend and her best friend. Could this day get any worse?

"Either take off your clothes and start fucking or get the hell out of my scene," Allen said.

"Sabrina, please," Brian said. "You can do better than this film. Chalice wants you sometime next month for a girl-on-girl film."

"I'm staying." She crossed her arms under her breasts and stuck her tongue out at him.

"I'm leaving," Sean said, heading for the door.

"You can't leave," she wailed. "I'm getting five grand for this."

"This?" Brian asked, looking around the hotel room for the first time. "You don't get paid five thousand for vanilla sex." He pinned Sean with a glare. "What were you going to do to her? Water sports?"

He had a vague idea what that was and fought to keep the revulsion off his face. "No. Nothing." Sean raised his hands in surrender. "She passed me a note saying I was going to audition for a porn role. Idiot that I am, I came here to see if I could find out why my sister died in this profession."

"It wasn't the profession."

"I get that now. The director told me to strip. When I came out of the bathroom, Sabrina was in bed. He wanted me to . . ." Sean realized he was talking about the man's girlfriend. ". . . engage in mutual oral stimulation."

Brian rolled his eyes. "That's one hell of an audition. What were you getting paid?"

"We didn't even discuss that yet."

That seemed to throw the other man. He looked around the room again, slower this time. Sean could see his eyes were calculating things Sean couldn't begin to understand. "Sabrina, what are you into?" Brian asked softly, his eyes finally narrowing on her.

Sabrina looked at the director. "Nothing. We weren't doing nothing but shooting a movie."

Brian walked over to the crew. "Who else was in the shoot?"

"No one," said the cameraman. "Just him. We're all getting paid top dollar."

"Who's paying for all this?" Brian asked Allen. "With the kind of money you're throwing around, you could have had named talent instead of a rookie with a medium-sized dick."

"Hey now," Sean said, checking that his wallet and keys were still in his pockets. He was ready to go. But before he could, Brian turned back to Sabrina.

"As a matter of fact, why him? You know a ton of actors who would jump at the chance for that kind of money."

"You are ruining everything." She stalked over to her boyfriend and swung at his jaw.

Brian sidestepped it and shoved her down.

Sabrina fell and started to sob. She curled into the fetal position.

"You're fine. I didn't push you that hard." Brian peered at her. "What is wrong with you?"

"She's on something," Sean said.

"On what?" Brian said.

"She's your girlfriend; you don't know if she's doing pot or meth?"

"What?" Brian crouched down to look at Sabrina, but she rolled away from him.

"Leave me alone," she cried. "I'm sorry I called you. I thought you'd have fun. You like to watch."

Sean was surprised that Brian didn't even seem remotely embarrassed that she was telling a room full of strangers that he got off on watching people have sex with his girlfriend. Then again, everyone in this room had been prepared to watch Sean fuck Sabrina.

"How do you know she's on something?"

"Her eyes are dilated."

"What did you do to her?" Brian turned to the director with his fist clenched.

"Nothing. She was like that when she came here." Allen looked pointedly at his watch. "I need someone to put her back on the bed and fuck the shit out of her. Which one of you is it going to be?"

"It's not the first time, either." Sean said, ignoring the director.

"What do you mean, not the first time?" Brian said.

"When we first started talking, I met her in the clinic where I work. She was high then, too."

"A clinic? Oh, shit," Brian said. He thought for a moment, and something seemed to click into place. "I think I know what's going on here. And you're not going to like it. Can you prescribe drugs?"

"I work with a nurse who does."

"She would give you anything you wanted," Sabrina said, sitting up. She wiped the fat, fake, tears away with the back of her hand. "You have that Gladys bitch wrapped around your finger. I heard the two of you. You recommend and she glows at you like a mother hen."

"I've heard enough," Brian said and walked over to the camera man. He wrested the equipment away and started deleting footage. "This is bogus. I'm making sure you guys don't have a single dick shot or anything to use against him."

"Stop him," the director said.

Sean covered Brian. "Let's not start something ugly. No one has to get hurt here." Sean cracked his knuckles and took up a fighting stance when one of the grips seemed to think about it. He stopped in his tracks when he realized Sean was serious about throwing punches.

"What's going on?" the cameraman asked, his hands in the air as though it was a stick up.

"Tell him who was bankrolling this project," Brian said, handing the camera back to its owner. He faced Allen.

Allen sighed. "He was." Allen pointed his chin at Sean.

"I was not. I would never. Hell, I don't even *have* the five thousand dollars she was offered." Sean jabbed a thumb at Sabrina.

"You wouldn't have paid in cash," Allen said.

"The drugs, Doc. The drugs," Brian said. "I'm out of here."

"You were going to blackmail me?" Rage reddened his eyes. "Were you blackmailing my sister?"

"Buddy, I don't know what you're talking about." Allen backed away from him.

Brian grabbed Sean's arm. "He's a lowlife. Desiree worked for legitimate studios."

"You can't go, Sean," Sabrina said. "You need to do this."

"Was my sister being blackmailed?" he asked Brian.

Brian snorted. "I doubt it. She'd have been tickled pink to have the exposure."

"But our parents . . ."

"Couldn't have stopped her even if they knew about it. Desiree didn't advertise that she fucked on camera, but she didn't hide from it either."

Like Liz. And Sarah.

Sean followed Brian out the door as Allen called out. "All right, let's not waste the set. Let's get somebody in bed. Sabrina, honey, put a cock in your mouth. I've wasted enough time today."

The ride in the elevator down was uncomfortable, to say the least. "So they were going to blackmail me for drugs?"

"Probably OxyContin."

"Jaysus," Sean said, blinking as he heard the brogue come out.

"Your sister. She was a good kid. I liked her. She had a girlfriend." Brian paused and looked meaningfully at him. "You understand what I'm saying."

Sean nodded. The blows just kept on coming. He pivoted, but didn't put his hands up. He deserved these punches for being an idiot.

"You have a problem with that?"

"No."

"She thought her family would disown her, if they knew anything about her life here. She didn't want them to know, but it wasn't a concern because she felt so distant from them."

"She told us she was doing odd jobs to make ends meet and we believed her," Sean said. "We didn't know anything about porn or the lifestyle, so it was easy to hear what she wanted to tell us."

"I filmed them a couple of times."

Sean cringed. This was real, though. This was what he wanted.

"They were beautiful. And I don't mean just physically. They loved each other. Their movies were more like erotic art. You should get it. There's a whole series of them out from Luscious Studios."

"I'll take your word for it," Sean grimaced. That was his sister Brian was talking about.

"You're not one of those assholes who think she turned gay because of the porn, right?"

"No," Sean said. He counseled enough teens through their fears about their sexuality to know people didn't "turn gay."

"I can give Laverne your number, if you want. I can't guarantee she'll call, but she might. She's grieving, too."

Sean fumbled around in his wallet until he came up with his business card. "I'd appreciate it."

As they were walking through the lobby, Sean risked one more question. "Did you know she was on drugs?"

Brian shook his head. "Sabrina or your sister?"

"Both. Either."

"Not a clue."

"I'm sorry about your girlfriend."

Brian looked up at the hotel. "Me, too."

Sean went straight to the gym. He didn't speak to anyone. He went to the locker room and suited up and then found McManus reading the Sunday comics and drinking coffee that smelled so acidic, it was made Sean's eyes water.

"You're full of piss and vinegar this afternoon."

"I'll spar with Donovan."

McManus looked up. "You sure about this, kid?"

"I'm ready."

"I can see that. But he ain't here. You want to beat the hell out of something, take it out on the bag. And if it's the other way around, you're not getting that here."

Sean beat the piss out of the training dummy and then pummeled the shit out of the heavy bag. He hit until he couldn't feel anything, couldn't think. There was only him and the rhythm of the boxing dance. He lost himself in it. The euphoria hit like a runner's high and he went at the speed bag while the adrenaline pumped through his veins.

After a while, the ache in his legs and arms punched through the haze. Sean slowed down, realized he was winded.

"I've got the hot tub all set up for you, kid," McManus said, supporting him back to the locker room. "You know, if you train like that every day, you'd have a shot at a heavyweight match."

"My life is so fucked up."

"Cry me a river, Perfessor, and get in the damn tub."

Sean dropped the gear and the rest of the clothes on the locker room floor and sank into the tub. He submerged his head and thought about not coming back up. But he did, pushing the long strands of hair away from his face.

"I'm not your goddamned nursemaid," McManus said.

"Leave it," Sean croaked out. "I'll get it later."

McManus continued to grumble while he put his gear away. "So what's your problem, firecracker?"

"Bad day." Sean let the jets pound water into his aching shoulders and back.

❊❊❊ ❊❊❊

When Liz's phone rang, she was hoping it was Sean. Every inch of her could still feel the impression of his lovemaking from last night. She could barely focus on the business card template she was reworking.

"Hello?" Liz hadn't recognized the number.

"Ms. Carter, this is Dr. Jenkins."

Liz smiled. "Did my paperwork go through all right? Is there anything else you need? I can run down there today. In fact, if you've got anything you'd like me to work on for next semester, I'd be glad to take a look and we can come up with a plan."

There was a long silence. "Ms. Carter, I'm afraid we're going to have to revoke the scholarship."

Liz laughed nervously. Was this a joke? "I'm afraid I don't understand."

"You weren't entirely honest in your application." Dr. Jenkins sighed.

"What are you talking about?" Liz snapped. "My credentials are real. I can back up every single one. . . ."

"Los Angeles, Ms. Carter. You left out your employment when you were in California. You said you did websites."

Dr. Jenkins's accusatory tone stiffened Liz's spine. "I did." She had a portfolio full of them. If she had to, she'd make a copy and run it down to the campus today.

"You failed to mention that you also were in porn."

Liz's stomach spasmed. Leaning back in her chair, she watched a spider crawl across the ceiling while she controlled her temper.

"That wasn't relevant to the job you were hiring for," Liz finally said, acid in her tone.

"I'm afraid we can't give you the scholarship." To give her credit, Dr. Jenkins did sound remorseful.

"Over something I did ten years ago?" Liz checked the urge to throw something at the poor defenseless spider. It was either him or her laptop. She snapped a pencil between her fingers instead to stem the rising tide of violence.

"Ms. Carter, I don't care about your checkered past. In fact, I don't care if you're currently hawking your wares on the Internet. I care because my department head got a DVD in his mailbox today. *Big, Busty, Beauties.*"

Liz closed her eyes and willed back the tears. *No. No. No.*

"The name Spice didn't ring any bells, and he was going to just write it off as a prank when the note spilled out that it was starring his new scholarship recipient. And it was only a matter of time and Google before he connected the two."

"Someone is trying to hurt me," Liz said.

"You should call the police."

"And say what? Someone is sending my old movies to people. That's not a crime." Liz's tears were flowing down her cheeks and her nose was stuffing up. "I have a nine-year-old boy. I'm trying to fulfill a dream. My past does not affect my work."

"It's affecting it now."

Liz smashed her hand down on her desk, upsetting her pen holder. Writing utensils went everywhere. "I can do the work study better than any of your candidates, and I'll do it with a high grade point average."

"I believe you would have, Ms. Carter. And for what it's worth, I am sorry. But our offer has been rescinded. Of course, you are welcome to attend NYU next semester, but the Bursar's office will be expecting a tuition payment. Good luck."

Liz glanced at the clock. She had three hours to fall apart, then she had to pick up Jonathan from school and carry on. After doing the ugly cry, Liz laid on the couch with a cold washcloth over her eyes. The snivels still shook her body from time to time, and each time she thought of the sheer malevolence of the person leaving those DVDs, new tears erupted.

The person knew her. That's what hurt the most. They could have gotten her address by following her. But the only people who knew about her scholarship were her friends or whoever they told. Why would anyone talk about her, though? Why would anyone hate her enough to do this?

Twenty-one thousand dollars a semester. It could as well have been twenty-one million. Hell, she was pretty sure twenty-one hundred was out of the question. Even if she broke it down, it still came out to be four thousand dollars a class. That was a lot of business cards and school posters.

See you soon.

Good. And God help you when you do.

Liz threw down the washcloth and sat up. She couldn't waste any more time feeling sorry for herself. So what if she wasn't going to get her psych degree? New dreams happened all the time.

Her phone buzzed and this time it was a text from Sean.

You are not going to believe the day I had.

"Bet mine is worse," she said, staring at the screen. If she told someone or wrote it down, it would become real. Liz wasn't ready for it to be real yet. She had until the end of January until she had to say anything. Maybe, she could convince Dr. Jenkins's boss to change his mind or maybe she'd land a corporate contract and earn sixty-thousand dollars a year.

Or maybe monkeys will fly out of my ass.

It would be so easy to tell Sean what happened. He'd commiserate and get all protective and angry and then he'd try to solve her problem, because that's what men did. She couldn't tell Sarah because she would blink at her and say, "Wipe your tears." And then she'd hand her a check for the tuition money.

She didn't want anyone to rescue her, damn it. She was doing a great job of rescuing herself until this bullshit came along.

She texted back. *Backed up with work. Come to the FATE meeting Monday at 8. CU then.*

Chapter Fifteen

*T*hank God, it's Monday.

She couldn't wait to see her friends and Sean, even though it was her self-exile that was partially causing her stress. Liz saw disapproving faces everywhere. She picked up Jonathan at school and swore someone was glaring at them through the classroom window. What would she do if a DVD showed up in the principal's office? That might actually be grounds to call the police. Liz groaned. She just wanted it to end.

At least she was ready to face her friends and Sean again. Hopefully, he could stay over and she'd make it up to him for being in such a funk. It wasn't easy giving up on her dream, so Liz decided not to. No matter how she crunched the numbers, though, they still sucked. Still, she was determined to squeeze out the four thousand dollars to take her Introduction to Psychology class for the spring semester.

Baby steps.

She also found that she didn't like not seeing Sean every day. Liz was regretting not including him in her plans this weekend. She and

Jonathan actually got out of the city and took the train down to New Haven to catch the Imagination Movers doing their show at the Long Wharf Theatre. Jonathan told her he was too big for them now, but he still begged for a Warehouse Mouse plushie. They stayed overnight at a nearby motel and got to tour the freedom schooner *Amistad* before heading back into the city. It had been good to get away and spend some time with Jonathan, even if he did con her into going to Ikea so he could have some Swedish meatballs. And if they hadn't had to take the train back, she probably would have bought another bookcase.

Sean was the first to arrive for the FATE meeting that night and, much to her surprise, Jonathan rushed him to get a hug in first.

"Hey, buddy," he said. "I got something for you." Sean handed him a gift bag that said Everlast on it.

"Oh boy, my own gloves," he pulled them out. "Mom, look!"

"Great, now he's never going to go to bed," Liz laughed.

Sean cringed. "Sorry."

"I'm just teasing." Liz came in for her hug, and if she held on too long, he didn't mention it. He smelled like spearmint and the cold October air. She wondered if anyone would notice if she stayed in his arms all night.

"I'm going to go put these in my room so you two can have some 'alone time.'" Jonathan emphasized the last two words and sped into his bedroom, shutting the door.

"Are you sure he's only nine?" Sean murmured in her ear.

"Nine going on nineteen." Liz sighed.

"Are you mad at me? Did I push too far the other night with the whole . . ." He curved his hand to cup her breast.

Liz bit her lip at the pleasure the contact gave her. She liked that he was now bold enough to touch her instead of avoiding the area like it might break. "No, just a rough week. I'll tell you later, but for right now, would you just kiss me until we're interrupted?"

"My pleasure."

As his mouth devoured hers, she hung on to her control for dear life. All she wanted to do was wrap her legs around him again and let him have his way with her. Or maybe she could have her way with him. Whatever. Both sounded good about now.

Sarah walked in, twirling her keys. "Well, don't mind me."

Liz didn't, and when Sean would have raised his head, Liz pulled him back down. Peter entered right behind Sarah.

"This is Sean, I take it."

Sean tried to break free, but Liz held up a finger to indicate she needed one more minute.

"Oh, take your time. I'm going to get a drink. And maybe an ice bucket. How long have the two of them been at it?" Peter asked.

"About five minutes," Jonathan said.

This time she let Sean pull away. She'd had enough to last her through the next couple hours until they were alone again. "Okay, we can take a hint. Sean, this is Peter."

"Nice to meet you." Sean shook Peter's hand.

Peter appraised him and said, "You'll do."

Liz went into the kitchen to get the snacks with Sarah while Peter gave Sean the third degree about his intentions toward Liz.

"He's so embarrassing," Liz said to Sarah.

"He's protective of you. We all are." Sarah gathered up the napkins and plates while Liz carried out the finger sandwiches and cookies. Jonathan snatched a chocolate chip even before the plate was on the table.

"That's the last one, Mister. You should go to your room soon."

"I want to say hi to Honey and Brian."

"All right." Liz ruffled his hair.

Brian came in next and stopped dead in his tracks in the doorway. Sean did a double take.

"Hey." Brian approached him. "What are you doing here?"

Sean let out a deep sigh. "I'm dating Liz."

"You two know each other?" Liz asked. She looked from one to the other. There was some strange tension in the air between them.

A woman knocked on the open door frame and peeked her head in. "Hello? Brian said it was okay for me to come."

"Oh, shit," Sean said.

Liz stared at him. It wasn't like Sean to be so rude.

"Uh guys, this is Sabrina," Brian said, moving away from the doorway.

Brian's girlfriend. He brought her. Liz put on a welcoming smile, but couldn't help noticing the room's tension grew thanks to the way Sean was glaring at Sabrina and the way Sabrina's face had grown red.

"Doc?" Sabrina said, shuffling in and closing the door behind her. "I'm really sorry about Thursday. I was a real shit. Please don't press charges."

Sean shook his head. "This isn't happening. Not like this."

"Press charges," Liz cut in. "What is going on here?"

"Liz, this isn't how I wanted you to find out." Sean turned to her, held her by the upper arms. "I tried to tell you a couple of times, but . . ."

"Tell her what?" Peter said.

"Why is this woman begging you not to press charges?" Liz squirmed free and backed away from him. A roaring in her head sounded like a freight train barreling toward her. She almost wanted to put her hands over ears to block out what was coming.

"I did a dumb thing," Sabrina said. "I don't want to go to jail."

"I'm not going to press charges," Sean said, turning back to Sabrina. "It was a mistake. On both our parts."

"What did you do?" Liz forced out. Her stomach was in knots. She couldn't handle another blow to her happiness.

"Sean was going to do a por—movie," Brian substituted, after noticing Jonathan was all ears. "With Sabrina. It was with an indie that had ulterior motives. I busted in and stopped it before anything happened."

"Nothing was going to happen. I was only there to . . ." Sean started to explain, but Sarah elbowed him hard in the ribs.

"Jonathan," Sarah said brightly. "Let's go in your room and play video games with the headsets on."

"What's going on?" Jonathan looked around the room.

Liz's heart broke for him. He really liked Sean.

I really liked Sean, too.

"Jonathan, please go with Sarah." Liz didn't think she was going to be able to handle this right now. She felt a freak out coming on and she didn't want Jonathan to see it.

"Okay," he said, taking Sarah's hand.

When Jonathan's door closed, everyone exhaled at once. Liz got her breath back first and rounded on Sean. "You were going to sleep with her?" She pointed to Sabrina.

Sabrina was everything Liz wasn't. Young, lithe, with taught skin and round, full breasts straining out of her scoop-neck sweater. Liz could easily see her splayed out on the bed with Sean's face buried between her . . .

"No," Sean said.

Liz snapped out of her hurtful daydream. It had seemed so real. For a moment, she'd been on the stage, feeling the lights and the noise of the crew. Only she had been an observer and very much aware of being an outcast.

"And he didn't," Sabrina said, pushing her long, honey blonde hair out of her eyes. "He just got naked for the director."

"Not helping," Sean told her with a vicious glare.

Sabrina shrugged and sank into the couch.

Liz looked between the two of them. There was a dynamic, a charisma, that the director would have loved. He was all fierce and dominant, and Sabrina could obviously project a waif-like innocence. Liz didn't buy her act for a minute. She could tell by the calculated looks Sabrina was flicking around the room that she was deciding how best to play this scene. *Sweetheart, this is not the audience you were expecting.*

Peter was literally gaping. At least he was sitting down, because otherwise Liz thought he'd be in danger of spilling his Evian all over the place. She wanted to stand next to him and watch the drama play out. Unfortunately, she was center stage.

Honey sailed in. "Sorry, I'm late. Traffic was dreadful." She peeled off her scarf. "Oh, we have some new faces."

Peter patted the couch next to him. "Have a seat, Honey. I'll catch you up later."

Brian put a supportive hand on Sabrina's shoulder. "She thought Sean would be the perfect leading man, but not for the reasons you think."

I just bet she did.

Sabrina might be warming Brian's bed, but Liz could see she had some interest in Sean.

"This was what you were trying to tell me?" Liz cried. "That you were getting back into the industry?"

"No. I was trying to tell you . . ." His eyes were clamped closed.

"Go away. Leave me alone," she said. She didn't want to hear the words. She didn't want to hear him say that he missed the sexual thrill or the power play or even the money. Liz had thought he was at the same point in his life that she was, and it blew her away that she let her hormones blind her to the fact. He was sexy and marketable. She should have known better. "I want you out of my apartment. Out of my life."

Sean's eyes flew open. She registered shock, hurt, and sadness, but she didn't care.

"I can't have Jonathan around this lifestyle anymore," Liz crossed her arms over her chest. "Not to mention I lost my scholarship to NYU because some asshole sent my advisor a copy of one of my movies. I'm trying to get them to accept me again. If they find out I'm dating a porn actor, my hopes are shot."

"I'm not a porn actor," Sean half laughed. "You don't understand."

No, she understood. She heard all the excuses before. *I only do one film a year* or *It's only part time, until I can get back on my feet,* or *I only work with people I know.* Liz shook her head. "I can't believe it. I thought you and I, well, that we had something. That we were on the same page." Liz heard her voice start to shake and she clamped her lips shut.

"Liz, we do have something." He took a step toward her. She backed away from him.

"Not if you can take a job screwing other women. There was a time when I could accept that type of relationship, but I can't now. Now, I think it's cheating."

"I never touched her," Sean said, flinging his hand at Sabrina.

"He didn't," Sabrina said.

"Would you both get out of my apartment? Brian, you stay."

"Liz, I know you're upset. And you have every right to be, but not about this." Sean gestured between Sabrina and himself. "There are things I need to tell you."

"Maybe," she said, wiping her eyes on her sleeve. "But I don't need to hear them. Now I know why I didn't want you meet the FATE group. I should have trusted my instincts. Deep down, I knew you weren't ready to leave the industry."

"That's absurd," Sean said. "You don't know what you're talking about." His hands balled into fists.

How dare he get mad at me.

"Why are you both still here?" Liz pointed toward the door.

"Sorry, baby." Sabrina kissed Brian on the cheek and slunk out. Liz couldn't decide if she wanted to applaud or throw her shoe. Sabrina was all sulky kitten.

"Liz, if you just give me a chance . . ." Sean stepped toward her again, but Peter was suddenly between them.

"Now's not the time," Peter said, putting a hand on Sean's elbow and tugging him away from her. "Tomorrow is another day."

Liz shook her head. "Don't call me. I'll call you when I'm ready. But don't hold your breath."

"Fine." Sean allowed Peter to lead him out.

Liz lasted until Peter closed the door on him and then she sunk down to the floor.

"Liz, I'm so sorry," Brian said. "But I'm confused."

"Join the club." Liz buried her head in her elbow and sobbed.

"You said Sean was a boxer and an ex-stripper." Brian sat down next to her and slung an arm around her.

"I don't want to talk about him right now," Liz said. "I am at the end of my rope." Her head was throbbing. It seemed like everything was going wrong. What was next? Cancer coming back? She groaned.

"Brian, this isn't important. Not now," Peter said.

"I think it is. You need to know that Sabrina was setting Sean up for a blackmail tape."

"Blackmail for what?" Liz pushed herself away from him and got to her feet. Where the hell were her tissues? She spotted them on top of the television armoire and grabbed a handful.

"This is where I'm missing something. The man that just walked out of here is Desiree Jones's brother," Brian said. "She's one of the actresses I used to film."

Liz held up her hand. "You knew Sean's sister, professionally?"

Brian nodded.

That would have meant she did lesbian porn. Sean's Catholic parents hadn't known she was a stripper, let alone a porn actress. "Sabrina was blackmailing Sean into not telling his parents about his sister? That sucks. But it doesn't change the fact he was looking for work."

"Sit down." Brian sat next to her on the sofa.

"I'm so stupid," Liz lamented.

"You're not stupid." Peter put his arm around her.

"It sounds like Sean was lying to you. That doesn't make you stupid. That makes him a ratfink." Honey's small frame shook with outrage.

"I'm still trying to sort all of this out," Brian said. "Sabrina does a lot of drugs. I don't think even she knows what she does. I never really knew how messed up she was until this week. She gave the director my number as a possible cameraman—not that I'd ever do it. But then she called me and I didn't like the sound of the operation. Strictly amateur hour. So I went to the hotel and it was a setup. They were going to film Sean and Sabrina and then bleed him for drugs."

"Sean isn't a drug dealer." Liz blew her nose. He was a lot of things, but she knew he wasn't that.

"He has access to them. Desiree always called her brother Doc when she talked about him because he worked in a clinic and was going for his PhD."

Sabrina called him that too when she walked in. Liz shook her head. "Sean is an undergrad and he works at a gym part time helping kids."

"I think that's a lie," Brian said. "Sabrina's been to his office. Spoke to his advisor nurse. Sabrina figured it was an easy way to get drugs."

"She sounds wretched, Brian," Honey frowned. "You deserve much better than that."

"I'm not defending her actions. She was high. She thought Sean would be into it."

Honey gave an unladylike snort.

"In her mind, Sean was lucky enough to do a porn with her and all he had to do was hand over some drugs. Wouldn't cost him a dime. Like I said, her head's not on straight."

Liz couldn't care less at the moment about Sabrina and her motivations. This whole dual life thing that Sean supposedly led was making her head spin.

"He still went to audition for a film." That was the unforgivable part. After spending a wonderful night in her bed, Sean got up the next morning and immediately was ready to have a go at some sexy, young thing who didn't have any hang ups or inhibitions.

Brian got up to pace the room. "Sabrina said he was torn up about his sister's death, that he wanted to know what drove her to the drug overdose that killed her."

Liz nodded. Sean's agony over his sister was too real to have been faked.

"I think he went there out of curiosity and then got in over his head." Brian crouched down next to her so he could look her in the eye. "He's a liar. But he's not a cheat."

"Well, that's a stunning recommendation," Honey said.

"I still don't know why he lied to begin with," Liz said in a small voice. "Did he think I was stupid? Was it fun for him to role-play with the porn star and then go back to his academic life?"

That was almost worse—to think he was laughing about her to his friends. She was nothing but a lab rat to him. What happens if we put the cheese down this maze? Only the cheese in his case was his cock. Fury whipped through her, burning out the sadness.

Peter knelt at her feet and took his hands in hers. "You're not stupid. He's not worthy of you. Forget him."

"Easier said than done," she said. It was easier to be angry than sad. Anger was empowering. She was going to be empowered by this situation.

Looking over her shoulder to confirm Jonathan's door was still closed, she said, "Boy, is Sarah going to be pissed she missed this." Something broke inside her, shattering into little pieces. She thought it must be her heart. But she had to soldier forth. She had her breakdown. It was time to put that on the back burner. "What am I going to tell Jonathan? And you," Liz said to Brian. "What are you doing with that horrible woman?"

Brian shrugged. "I love her."

"She's a drug addict, a reckless porn actress, and a blackmailer." Honey ticked off the items on her fingers.

"No one's perfect."

Liz gave a watery chuckle.

"Besides, when we're together, she makes me feel complete." Brian smiled. "We can work on everything else."

"You're a better man than me," Peter said. "I'd like to bang both their heads together for hurting Liz."

"Brian, do you think Sabrina is the one who has been sending my DVDs all over the place?" Liz asked.

Brian shook his head. "She doesn't even know who you are. I figured if she fit in with the group, she'd find out then."

"Are you sure?"

"Positive. If you weren't at last year's AVN convention, she doesn't think you exist."

Holly poured the tea and handed Liz a cup. "You lost your scholarship, huh?"

Liz accepted it, gratefully. The fragrant brew soothed her with its warmth and familiarity. "It's been a bad week."

"Do you think Sean's been doing it?" Holly asked. "These DVDs never showed up until he arrived. He knows where you live and knows the campus."

"Why would he be so cruel?" Liz's lips were quivering again. She had to put the teacup down before she dropped it.

"Maybe he wanted revenge for his sister?" Holly helped her bring the cup to the table.

"I didn't even know his sister. That's just . . . it's too horrible to think about." Liz had opened up to him and, if this was true, he deliberately sent her movie to her advisor and he might as well have punched her in the kidneys.

Chapter Sixteen

It had only been three days, but they were the longest, emptiest days of his life. Even the first few days after Mary Katherine's death didn't feel this bad. Sean was going through the motions, putting on a façade for the world, only the part he was playing wasn't stripper/boxer; it was himself. He didn't like it. He missed Liz in little ways, like when he saw a funny sign he wanted to send her a picture of so she'd laugh, or when he was alone in his bed, or pretty much every other time of the day.

He called, but it went to voice mail. He sent a text and it was ignored. Sean stopped trying. He spent hours composing a long email explaining everything. But in the end, he deleted it, unsent. It seemed too selfish to give his side without her input. Besides, the last thing he wanted her to think was that he was stalking her. He went through every last bit of that conversation, analyzing every sentence and beat. He should have interrupted and talked over her—anything so that she didn't think he would ever sleep with someone else the morning after they made love, that we would cheat on her.

She hated him for all the wrong reasons.

What does it matter? She hates me and I deserve it.

When Sean's phone rang, his stupid heart started to pound, thinking it was Liz. Even if she was calling to tell him off, he wanted to hear her voice and try again to tell her the truth.

I fucked up.

I love you.

But it was a number he didn't recognize. Sean answered it anyway. "Yeah?"

"Is this Sean O'Malley?" a woman with a trace of an Irish accent asked. One of his mother's friends? He couldn't peg the age.

"Who wants to know?" He pressed the print button for his mainframe download. Sean was looking at a long day of analysis. The prospect didn't thrill him as much as it usually did.

"My name is Laverne. I was your sister's lover."

She said it quietly, with dignity and with a hint of challenge in her voice, as if she expected him to argue.

"I'm so glad you called. Can you meet for coffee?" Life began stirring in him again.

"Why don't you come over for dinner tonight around five? I made lasagna. Your sister said it was your favorite."

Words choked him, but he managed to get one out: "Okay."

She gave him her address and then hung up. He stared at it. Chelsea—Hell's Kitchen prior to renovation—the same neighborhood where his sister lived, although a nicer area if he recalled correctly. Sean wiped his arm across his desk to dump all the paperwork into his backpack and hurried home to shower and shave.

At 4:59, the doorman let him into a large apartment building and keyed the elevator that led straight up to the apartment. Laverne was waiting for him. She had strawberry blonde curls down past her shoulders and a spattering of freckles across her nose. Pale green eyes assessed him as he handed her a double magnum bottle of cabernet sauvignon.

"What if I didn't like wine?" she asked with a faint smile and a hint of Irish in her voice.

"That's for me. I don't know what you're drinking," he said.

"Oh no, you have to share. Let me take your coat."

Sean shrugged out of his leather jacket and handed it to her. Looking around as she hung up his coat and brought the wine to the small table set up in the living room, he saw it was a well-furnished two bedroom apartment with a view of Midtown.

"Here, let me," he said when he noticed she was struggling with the corkscrew.

He opened the bottle and poured two full glasses.

"We should let this breathe," she said. "Are you hungry?"

"A little." He took a deep breath. "It smells really good in here."

Following her into the kitchen, he stared at the pictures on the refrigerator while she checked on the lasagna. There were a few of Mary Katherine mugging for the camera. He swallowed hard, but a tremulous smile formed. Touching the one where she was giving duck lips at some nightclub, he wondered if Sabrina had taken that picture seconds before they ran out on the men liquoring them up.

"Has Sabrina been around?"

Laverne shuddered. "I don't have anything to do with the toxic little bitch. She's a drama factory. If drama doesn't exist, she'll manufacture it. Desiree and Sabrina often worked together. Sometimes, we all hung out. I tolerated her for Des's sake, but now it's just too much effort to remain in contact with her."

Sean could understand. Sabrina was a bit of a nightmare. He ran his hand through his hair and pointed to a picture of Mary Katherine and Laverne with chef hats on. They were in an industrial kitchen, all sparkling stainless steel.

Laverne was watching him, her eyes shiny with tears. "We took some cooking classes at Le Cordon Bleu. We were pretty good." She wiped her face with the kitchen towel. "We were going to have you over for dinner. It just never happened."

"My fault," Sean said. "I should have made it a priority."

"It's not your fault." Laverne tossed down the dish towel. "We thought we'd get out of the business first. Then it wouldn't be 'meet my girlfriend, we do porn together.' Although, Des thought you probably wouldn't hear anything after 'girlfriend,' so she thought it would be fine to do it sooner."

Sean looked away, his eyes cataloging everything in the apartment.

"You looking for something?" she asked. "We keep the sex toys in the bedroom." Laverne's voice was flat and vicious.

"Where do you keep the drugs?" Sean returned the favor.

To his surprise and chagrin, the tears she had been holding back began to flow in earnest and great big sobs shuddered through her. His first reaction was to walk out and go to the gym and hit something hard. But if Mary Katherine had loved her, she would have be ashamed of him if he did.

"I'm sorry. Please don't cry." He looked around for tissues before handing her the kitchen towel.

Laverne got herself under control after a few minutes. "The lasagna should be done. Why don't you go sit down?"

And go fuck yourself.

Sean finished the sentence in his head for her. He sat at the table, taking a healthy swig of the wine. Completely aerated or not, it soothed his temper as it went down. He was mad at only himself.

A text came through and he fished his phone out of his pants to see who it was. It was Liz. All the air exited the room. His fingers shook when he thumbed to the message.

RU still coming as Prinz Charming????? 2morrow @8 B there or B []

Jonathan had gotten his hands on his mother's phone.

Yes.

Let her call or text him back and tell him not to come if she wanted to. Of course, now he had to figure out how to get a prince costume the night before Halloween. Hell, he was in New York City, he should be able to find something. Google was a lifesaver. He looked up from his phone when a plate of steaming hot lasagna was put in front of him. Laverne's portion was more moderately sized.

"What are you looking up?"

He told her and she laughed. It sounded like bells ringing. If it was true that an angel gets its wings every time a bell rang, maybe Mary Katherine was fluttering nearby.

"Do you have blue pants—not jeans—and a white shirt?"

Sean narrowed his eyes in thought. "Sweatpants, yeah."

"Go to the fabric store tomorrow and buy a few yards of gold rick rack and glue them up and down the outside of the legs. You got a sword, right?"

"Uh, no." He picked up his fork and tried to decide how to shovel a mouthful in without burning his tongue. Settling on blowing at it, he looked up at Laverne expectantly.

"Well, get one. You can't be Prince Charming without a sword."

He put down the fork to make a note on his phone: *riftraft,* whatever the hell that was, *sword . . .*

"Your regular belt should work. Just wear it over your shirt. You're going to need epaulets."

"I am?"

"You can make them out of white cardboard and glue them on your shoulders."

glue, white cardboard . . .

"A sash. A large gold sash. And you should be done." Laverne beamed and tucked into her side salad.

Oh yeah, he hadn't noticed there was a nice green salad. He ate that first to be polite and because the inside of the lasagna was still molten.

"Thank you for inviting me," he said, trying to make up for his earlier bluntness.

"I wish it had been while she was still alive."

"Laverne," he put down his fork. "Why did she die?"

It was the question his heart had been asking for more than three months, but it was the first time it came out of his mouth.

Laverne took a long swallow of wine. "I ask myself that all the time."

"When did she start using?"

Laverne shook her head. "She didn't. Not really. She was always chasing a new thrill, a new experience. I know she tried drugs before but didn't like them. Marijuana made her hungry and sleepy. Cocaine bounced her off the wall. The ice was a new thing. I saw the pipe, but she was always buying edgy paraphernalia like that. I didn't think she was smoking anything." Laverne rolled her eyes and took another deep swallow of wine. "She used to tell off the crew who went outside to smoke. 'You're ruining the air . . .'"

"'For all of us,'" Sean mimicked his sister's voice.

"Exactly." Laverne saluted him with her glass.

"Why didn't you come to the funeral?" he asked.

"I did. I stayed in the back. I waited until you all had left."

"You could have introduced yourself. Said you were a friend."

"I wasn't just her friend." Laverne slammed down her fork. "And I wasn't going to pretend otherwise to a bunch of self-righteous assholes who would have told me my wife was going to hell."

"Wife?" Sean croaked.

Laverne waved her hand wearily. "We never had the chance to make it legal. But it was another thing we were going to do. And now we never will." She looked down at her plate and started toying with her lasagna.

Sean drank wine because he didn't know what to say.

"Brian told me you thought porn drove her to the drugs," Laverne said when the silence became too much.

"No," Sean said. "I didn't know. I convinced myself the lifestyle led to drug abuse, but three months of analysis with NYU's finest computers and I can't find any correlation that doesn't exist in other professions as well."

He thought of Sabrina's comment about stockbrokers and it was true; they scored in the highest percentile of drug users in the workplace.

"Brian also told me that Mary Katherine was very happy in her chosen profession and with you," Sean said.

"I'd like to think so." Laverne stared out into the living room. "What do your parents know about her death and her life?"

"They don't know about the stripping, or the porn, or you."

Laverne's smile resembled a grimace. "Their little baby got swallowed up by the Big City?"

Sean nodded. "I can see that's where they're slanting the truth to be."

"Are you going to tell them the real truth?" she glared at him.

"No. It serves no point. My parents wouldn't believe it anyway."

"They should know that what we had wasn't a sin or disgusting. It was beautiful. We loved each other." Laverne was crying again, and this time he pushed his chair back and went over to her.

After an awkward moment, he hugged her. And after another awkward pause, she hugged him back. While they comforted each other, the lasagna cooled down and the tears dried up. Sean resumed his seat and poured two more glasses of wine.

"I'm glad you brought the big bottle," she said.

"I planned ahead."

"Des said you were a Boy Scout. She was proud of everything you accomplished. She thought your dad drove you too hard."

Sean shrugged. "It was his way."

"Was it tough growing up with him?"

Sean sighed and dug into his lasagna. "It wasn't a picnic." Flavors exploded in his mouth, the creamy ricotta and the smoky mozzarella. The sauce was fresh and bits of meats and sausage dotted throughout it. "This. Is. Amazing," he said around a mouthful.

"It was Des's favorite."

Sean chewed and swallowed. "You never call her by her real name?"

"Desiree was her real name. She hated Mary Katherine." Laverne sipped her wine, shooting him a challenging look over the glass.

He blinked. Took another big bite, savored it. "I didn't know that."

"There's a lot of things you didn't know." Glancing down at her plate, she sighed. "And now it's too late."

Sean leaned back in his chair. "I'm sorry for that. I wish I could change things, but I can't. I am happy that my sister had a nice life. She seemed like she was happy."

Laverne dabbed at her eyes. "I'd like to think so."

"She wouldn't have been satisfied to stay on Long Island."

"Not with your parents anyway." Laverne gave a half laugh.

"Even without them. Manhattan was her city. She belonged here. She belonged with you." Sean tapped his wine glass to hers.

"Are you going to pretend I didn't exist and that she didn't fuck on camera for money?" Laverne challenged.

"I'm not going to dwell on the 'fucking' part. Eww, that's my sister you're talking about. But no. As far as I'm concerned, you are my sister-in-law." Sean finished his wine.

"But I'm a lesbian." Laverne regarded him with narrowed eyes.

"Which is why you're not my brother-in-law." He refilled his glass and topped off hers.

"I thought your people have a problem with my people." Laverne waggled her fork back and forth between them.

"I'm a therapist. We're all people. We all make mistakes. Some of us regret them for the rest of our lives." He thought of Liz. "Some of us die from them." He shook his head. "What a fucking waste. I'd like to smash that pipe over Mar—Desiree's thick head."

"Get in line," Laverne said, and then attacked her lasagna with gusto.

They made quick work of the rest of the meal and took their wine into the comfy chairs that looked out over the city.

"What are you going to do?" he asked. "Are you still going to make movies?"

"Nah," she shook her head. "Too much hassle. I've got a webcam set up in the bedroom. I cut out the middle man. I have a subscription service. I do webcasts and interviews. Every Monday is a guest feature."

"If you don't mind asking, how much . . ."

"Enough to pay for this apartment every month and to live decently in the greatest city of the world." Laverne primped her hair and gave him a sassy grin.

"Holy shit," he said. "I thought when I made five hundred dollars a night it was top dollar."

"What?" Laverne goggled at him.

So he told her all about dancing at Club 69. And, of course, that led into FATE and Liz. Pretty soon he was drinking more wine and telling Laverne all about his stupid ideas.

"Just because I thought I could be like Margaret Mead in Samoa." He slapped his hand against his forehead. "I'm such a jackass. I forgot the rules. Shadowing, cultural immersion, minimum impact. All out the fucking window. Bottom line is that we're all people and we're all some type of fucked up inside. And now I lost the best thing in my life because I was an arrogant jerk."

"You need to tell her that," Laverne said.

"I tried. She hates me." The wine was making him maudlin and he was half aware that he was on his way to a good drunk.

Another text buzzed in his pants. If it was Liz telling him not to bother, he was going to toss his phone in the trash. But it wasn't. It was McManus.

You're inked for Kyle Donovan. Be at the gym Saturday 7 am.

"Seven a.m.?"

"Isn't that still the middle of the night?" Laverne said.

"On a Saturday no less?"

Laverne winced. "What could possibly be worth being somewhere at that hour?"

"I'm going to be a sparring partner for an up-and-coming heavyweight. I guess that's when the professionals train. I love getting up early on my day off to get the shit kicked out of me."

"You could have said no."

Sean shook his head. "Nah, I'll take my lumps. It's penance."

"You Catholics are weird."

"It's genetic," Sean said. "Well, I should get going. Thank you for a lovely dinner." He got up, staggered a bit as the room tilted. He risked falling on his ass by leaning down and kissing her cheek.

"Why don't you stay here for a while? Just until you sober up."

"Nope," he said. "I've got to find riff raff for my costume tomorrow. I want to impress Liz."

"Wait," Laverne stood up. "She's going to be at the costume party?"

"Yup. Her son just asked me if I was still going. He's going to be a Power Ranger. But Liz is going to be dressed as Cinderella."

"You didn't tell me this was hardcore."

Sean blinked. "Is that an industry term? Because I'm not taking my pants off again."

"Oh yes, you are. I'll need to sew the rickrack on them. I originally came to New York to do costumes and backstage work. I wasn't that good. And porn pays better. But I can hook you up with a Prince Charming costume."

"I guess this makes you my fairy godmother."

"I'm going to pretend you didn't say that." Laverne handed him his jacket and spun him out the door. She locked up and followed.

Chapter Seventeen

Liz wiggled her toes in her sneakers and tried not to feel like she was cheating. No one would know or care that she wasn't wearing glass slippers under the big blue dress, but it still felt wrong. She put a cautious hand up to her blonde wig to make sure it was holding up.

"You look beautiful, Mom," Jonathan said.

He had been so excited to see her in her costume. He even made her put on makeup and go all out.

"No one is going to be looking at me, sweetheart. They're all going to be wondering who the brave Red Power Ranger is."

Jonathan struck a pose and Liz fake shivered. The school was decorated like a haunted house, with black crepe paper and cotton ball spider webs. The cafeteria was set up like a club with the tables on the far sides so the center was the dancing. The DJ was playing oldies like "The Purple People Eater" and the tamer versions of some of Dr. Demento's favorites.

Jonathan spotted his friends. They were dressed as mummies, ninja turtles, and a green-hatted elf that was either Link or Legolas, but Liz wasn't sure. Looking around, she saw some mothers she knew, but as she made her way over to them, they split up and went in different directions. Changing course herself, she got a glass of orange punch and a cookie from the table.

"Did you make these?" she asked one of the teachers, who smiled coldly and walked away.

What the hell was wrong with everyone? Didn't they know she just wanted a fun night out with some adult conversation? One where she didn't spend her time analyzing Sean's every single word and action since the moment they first started chatting online. There'd been clues, she admitted. And, to give him credit, he did try and start conversations. In her defense, though, Liz had thought they were about his sister's death and not about the revelation of his big, fat lies. But maybe she should have let him finish instead of jumping his bones. He listened to her confession about Jonathan's existence, after all. Feeling very much an outcast, Liz walked the decorated halls to her son's classroom to admire all the work on the walls. She sought out his stuff and was pleased to see his handwriting was neat and that his recycle poster was done on the computer. Impressed, Liz headed back toward the main area. Maybe she would find an alcove and text Sarah.

"Liz Carter! I was hoping you were going to be here."

Liz smiled. Finally, someone wanted to talk to her. Unfortunately, she didn't recognize the man coming toward her. He was dressed like the devil, which wasn't easing her nerves any, but what really scared her was not the red-horned costume with the barbed tail. No, it was the fact that he carried a DVD case.

Now she really wished she had glass slippers so she could smash them on his head.

"I'm a really big fan. Would you sign this for me? My son's in your son's class. Luke." The devil pointed and, sure enough, a little angel was talking with Jonathan. They seemed oblivious.

Liz took the pen he handed her, thinking it could be used as a weapon. Of all the things Sean never got around to explaining, self-defense was at the top of the list. "I'm surprised you recognized me," she said, accepting the DVD from him.

"I didn't." He beamed at her. "Renee told me."

"Renee?" Liz asked.

"The school secretary."

"Mrs. Pierce?" she shrieked.

"She didn't recognize you either. Not at first. It was your friend, Sugar. She's not here, too, is she?" A lecherous look came over him as he scanned the room. He chuckled, a low and dirty sound. "I'd give my left nut to get a picture with her."

"Mrs. Pierce recognized Sar—Sugar?"

Liz had introduced Sarah to Mrs. Pierce as Sarah Canning. Closing her eyes, Liz saw her mistake. It had been all over the papers who Cole Canning married. Mrs. Pierce just needed to put together the pieces.

"Did you leave a DVD at my door? And send one to my school?" she accused the man.

"Huh? No. I figured we'd run into each other sooner or later. So, are you alone?"

Before Liz could jab him with the pen, a deep, familiar voice from behind her said, "No."

Luke's dad looked up and laughed. "Well, I see your prince has come. Have fun tonight." He waggled his eyebrows. "You lucky dog."

Liz scribbled her name and handed it back to the disgusting man. It was the quickest way to get rid of him. She didn't dare turn around.

"What are you doing here?" Liz whispered once Luke's dad sauntered away out of earshot.

"Haven't checked your text messages lately?"

Sean's voice was dry and she could feel the heat coming off his body. Part of her wanted to melt into his warmth and strength, the other part of her was telling her to grow a pair. She decided to look through her old texts instead.

"Jonathan," she sighed. "He doesn't understand."

"Actually, neither do you. I wanted . . ."

She held up her hand. "I know who you are, Doc."

Now it was his turn to sigh. "Not yet, but I am going for the PhD."

Liz whirled on him. "What was truth and what were lies?" She jammed her hands onto her hips, but the sight of him wilted her. He looked exactly like Prince Charming. Right down to the details.

"How did you . . . Was it your neighbor the party planner?"

Not fair. It was bad enough she was so attracted to him, but as Prince Charming to her Cinderella? Defenseless. She circled around him, touched the gold sash. God, what a role-play night they could have had. Her fingers were aching to touch the strong line of his back where the white jacket was stretched tight.

"Desiree's partner, actually. I had dinner with her last night. We went over a lot of things." Sean reached to hold her hand and bring her back to face him. She let him take both of her hands in his.

Liz wore gloves, but his heat scorched through the satin.

"I lied about my job and my level of education," Sean said. "Everything else was true. I'm so very sorry I hurt you. It wasn't my intention. Things just got out of hand and complicated. I handled everything wrong. Please forgive me."

"Did you really strip? You didn't get a buddy at Club 69 to vouch for you?" She pulled her hands away, folded them across her chest.

"For a whole week." He left her to walk over to the refreshment table.

She watched him, her Prince Charming. He was charming a few teachers with his sexy smile, but he didn't stay and press his advantage. Almost immediately, he came back carrying two glasses of punch. She missed the view of his ass in those pants, but the front was pretty special, too.

"I don't believe you actually stripped at Club 69." Liz took the proffered cup and they walked together toward the cafeteria.

"I could show you." He gave her a sexy smile.

Yes, please. I mean. No. Go to hell. After.

Happily ever after?

"Argh," she said, turning away from him and crossing her eyes. "You make me crazy. I'm pissed at you."

"You have every right to be. But tonight, let me be your bodyguard in case any other creepers come out of the woodwork." He held out his elbow. "It's the least I can do."

She was weak. He was Prince freaking Charming after all. And she was Cinderella.

"Just for tonight. We're not back together."

"I understand, but maybe we could still be friends."

Liz bit her lip. "I don't think so. I trust my friends."

"How about just for tonight?"

She took his elbow. "All right."

"Sean! Sean! You came!" Jonathan ran up to them.

"You, Mister, are in big trouble," Liz said, attempting to sound stern. "You know you're not allowed to touch my phone."

"Sorry, Mom," he said, looking anything but. "Sean, are you coming home with us?"

"No," Liz said. What a question. Mortification flooded her. Didn't Jonathan realize what would happen if he came home? No, of course not. He was only nine. He probably thought they'd stay up all night and play video games. Liz wanted to play games with Sean all right, but they were more along the lines of Prince Charming ravishing Cinderella at the ball.

"I'll walk you home," Sean said. "It's a dark night out there."

Liz's face flushed. *What would the harm be?* a sneaky voice inside her said. Her heart still hadn't recovered from the last go-round. Not a good idea. She wouldn't let him in. If Sean stepped foot inside her apartment dressed like that, she'd never forgive herself if she didn't indulge in a little fantasy.

"Cool, we can talk then." Jonathan slipped back into the dance. They were doing the Time Warp from *The Rocky Horror Picture Show.*

"I'm not dancing with you," Liz told him. That would weaken her resolve in a heartbeat.

"Okay."

He didn't have to sound so agreeable. Liz could have used a good fight to get her mind off him ravishing her. As it was, she knew what her next fantasy was going to entail. Then out of the corner of her eye, she saw someone else she needed to get mad at.

"Mrs. Pierce," Liz called out to the school secretary. "Can I have a word with you?" She dragged Sean with her. It wasn't for moral support, but she didn't feel so alone with him next to her.

Renee Pierce was standing with the assistant principal, who turned eight shades of red when he saw her and darted away before she got into conversation distance.

"Another fan," Liz muttered.

"What is it, Ms. Carter?" she sneered the *Ms.*

"Did you put one of my movies outside my door with the note that said, 'See you soon'?"

Liz felt Sean tense beside her.

"Why would I do that? It was probably one of your fans." Apparently she had a habit of sneering the last words of every sentence.

"Except, no one knew who I was until you recognized Sarah."

"You mean Sugar?" Mrs. Pierce said. "My ex-husband used to watch you girls all the time. Didn't you do a scene together?"

"Looks like you watched, too." Liz smiled. "It wasn't my best work. Sarah is god-awful at girl-on-girl. It's not my strong area either. Mine's blow jobs. Or anal play. What do you think, dear?"

She pierced Sean with a look.

"I can't pick," he said with a shrug.

Mrs. Pierce was not even trying to contain her disgust as she looked at them.

"Did you send the DVD to NYU?" Liz asked. She was pretty sure, but she wanted confirmation.

A flash of triumph flickered in the secretary's eyes. "NYU has standards. If they found out how you spread your legs for a living, don't blame me. They'll give the scholarship to someone more deserving. Maybe someone who has worked years in education instead of on her back."

"You applied for it, too, huh? And it was more on my knees than on my back." Liz understood now. It was never a stalker or Sean—she felt a flash of guilt that she even considered he could be so hurtful. It was someone who wanted to get a little dig in because her ex-husband liked pornography and, as a bonus, had found a way to take out the competition. If Liz had known it was going to come to this, she wouldn't have been so chatty with the school secretary. "Did you get it? The scholarship, that is."

"I haven't heard." Mrs. Pierce sniffed and turned her back on them. "Please excuse me. I have other people to speak with."

"Better hope you don't," Liz told her.

"Don't you threaten me," Mrs. Pierce said, whirling back. "Every teacher and most of the parents know about you. You're not going to have a leg to stand on if you accuse me of anything."

Poor Jonathan. She hoped he'd be a little older before all this started up.

"I wasn't threatening." Liz leaned in close. "It's a damn promise. I've got friends with mad editing skills. You're going to star in a DVD of your own."

"Anyone who knows me knows I would never do a pornographic movie."

"Sister," Sean said. "You ain't got the looks or the class for it."

"Whoremonger," Mrs. Pierce spat at him.

"Bitch," he said back.

"You go to hell." She shook her finger at him. They were beginning to attract attention.

"Sean," Liz gently pushed him back. "Don't engage with people like her. Renee, I'm sorry your husband would rather watch porn that be with you."

"Ex-husband," she breathed between her teeth.

"But if it wasn't me, it would have been someone else. You violated my privacy. You made me frightened that I had a stalker and you cost me a twenty-thousand-dollar scholarship. What the hell did I ever do to you? I have a nine-year-old boy. I work my ass off doing posters for this school, *gratis*. And this is the thanks I get? Cold shoulders and leering looks? Fuck you. Fuck all of you."

Liz stalked away, her pretty blue gown swirling with her. Sean, bless him, didn't miss a beat and kept up with her. "Let's find Jonathan," she said. "We're leaving."

"No, we're not." Sean guided her toward the dance floor.

"I want to go home." Liz tugged on her arm. She was riled up enough to allow herself to have angry sex with Sean.

Or have another good cry.

No, damn it, I am sick of crying.

And if I get into bed with him, I might never get out.

"I changed my mind," Liz grabbed his arm. "Sean O'Malley, you owe me a dance."

It was safer that way.

There weren't a lot of slow Halloween songs, so Liz wasn't tempted to cling to his broad shoulders and bury her face in his chest. But they danced to "Love Potion Number Nine" and Jonathan joined them for "Witch Doctor." The night ended with Heart's "Magic Man," but Liz heard another one of their songs in her head.

"What about Love?"

"This wasn't as bad as I thought it was going to be," Liz admitted as they gathered up all their props and belongings. A few parents made it a point to thank her for the raffle tickets and the posters. Maybe they didn't know she was the infamous Spice. Maybe they did. In the end, she was Liz Carter, mother of Jonathan Carter.

"You showed them that they can't hurt you," Sean said, slipping his arm around her.

"They can," Liz said darkly. "But only if they go after him."

Jonathan was finishing up trading candy with his friends.

"Do you think they will?" Sean's grip tightened.

Liz liked the solidarity in his touch. "If they do, it will probably be more on a peer-to-peer level." She didn't like to think that Jonathan was going to be teased and bullied because of her. She'd have to prepare him for the worst of it and hope he wouldn't grow to hate her for her choices.

On the walk home, Liz was grateful for the darkness. It hid her face so Jonathan couldn't see how worried she was. "Jonathan? Did you have a good time tonight?"

"Yeah, I think Brenna deserved the best costume prize."

Brenna went as a Weeping Angel from *Doctor Who*. It was a statue that came to life and grabbed you if you looked away or blinked. *Yeah, thanks for the nightmares, Brenna.*

"And Kendell was the funniest."

Kendell went as a yellow minion from *Despicable Me*. It was his fart gun that put him over the top. Liz must have told Jonathan five times that he couldn't have one.

"Are you sad that you didn't win a prize?" Sean asked.

"No, but they didn't have a 'badass' category." Jonathan struck a martial art pose.

"Jonathan Elliot Carter," Liz snapped. "Language."

"Sorry, Mom."

"You know why kids have middle names, don't you Jonathan?" Sean said, slipping his hand over Liz's.

She let him entwine his fingers with hers. The dark night also hid the rush of pleasure she got from his touch. Liz was going to need the reassurance in a few moments—just as soon as she got up enough courage to talk to Jonathan about her former career.

"Elliot is my grandfather's name," Jonathan said.

"It's so that kids know when they're really in trouble. *Ba dum dum.*" Sean made a drum and cymbal noise.

Jonathan laughed his goofy laugh. "I thought you guys should have won cutest couple."

"Oh, I don't know. Raggedy Ann and Andy were pretty deserving," Liz said. They put a lot of work in their costumes, too. The red yarn hair wigs were over the top. Of course, her own beehive was ready to fall down after dancing for an hour straight. *Okay, they were almost home.* She wanted the dark to cover her face in case he made her cry. She squeezed Sean's hand.

"I wanted to let you know that some kids at school might start teasing you about Mommy," Liz said in a rush.

"What for?" Jonathan thought she didn't know he was rooting around in his goodie back for candy, but Liz let it pass.

"Before you were born, Mommy was an actress. I made movies without any clothes on."

"Yeah, I know."

"What do you mean you know?" Liz snarled.

Sean held her arm and even Jonathan looked taken aback. If that bitch Mrs. Pierce showed her son a DVD, Liz was going to have her arrested so fast her head would spin.

"I hear you and Sarah talking all the time."

Oh. It was her big mouth and his big ears.

"Well, I want you to be prepared for it. If kids start to bully you, you need to tell me right away and I'll take it up with the principal. Hell, I'll go to the superintendent if that doesn't work. Whatever you do, don't go to Mrs. Pierce."

"Why?"

"I don't trust her."

"Okay," Jonathan slipped his hand into hers. "You don't have to worry about me, Mom."

For just this moment, she let herself be in the moment. Her two favorite men were holding her hands, and the tickling at the back of her throat might be happiness. When she started to dream of forever, she dropped Sean's hand.

They climbed the five flights of stairs up to her apartment. Liz was grateful for her sneakers. If she still had her Louboutins, her feet would be crying *no más* about now.

"Go inside. Get on your pajamas. Brush your teeth. And get in bed. I'll be right in," Liz said.

"Is Sean coming in?"

"Not tonight, buddy," he said.

The smile faded from Jonathan's face. "Goodnight," he mumbled.

Liz closed the door to give them privacy—or as much privacy as they could get in a landing.

"I could stay, if you wanted me to," he said.

She shook her head. She was so damned tempted. "I don't sleep with strangers."

"I deserved that," he said. "It sounds like you found out who was harassing you. Are you going to take it up with the school board?"

"If it continues," Liz said. "Right now, I'll just start a timeline and put it in writing for my own records. If Jonathan starts being targeted, I'll at least have proof to fall back on." She tugged on her gloves. Her hands were starting to sweat.

"He's a great kid."

Liz nodded.

"Is there any way I can fix this? I miss you." Sean slowly unbuttoned her gloves. He pressed a kiss on the exposed flesh each button revealed. Liz leaned back against the door and let him. When he finally tugged them off, she was ready to do the same thing with her panties. There was definitely a fantasy in here. Prince Charming debauching Cinderella at the ball. Her lips twitched. It would make a great porno. Instead of going around fitting slippers, he could go around . . . her smile faded.

"I want to be in your life," Sean said. "Liz, I love you."

She closed her eyes. "Don't."

"This isn't a lie. Not what we have between us." He brushed a black curl that had escaped from her wig off her forehead.

"I don't know that, Sean. You made me doubt everything."

"Liz, you are the strongest woman I know. You are smart and sexy and I fucked it all up. If you give me another chance, I'll never lie to you again."

"I want to believe you." Her heart was aching with the need to just jump into his arms again. "I need some time."

Sean's smile lit up his whole face. "I can do that."

He leaned in and it took all the willpower she possessed to turn her head so he got her cheek.

Chapter Eighteen

M om, can I still take boxing lessons?" Jonathan asked the next morning at breakfast.

Liz should have known this was coming. "I don't think that's such a good idea," she said. It was too early to have this conversation. She hadn't even had her coffee yet. She fixed it and sat down at the table with him.

"I promise I won't get hurt." He poured himself a bowl of cereal and doused it with almond milk.

It's not you I'm worried about.

Liz knew that if she took Jonathan to the gym every Wednesday, it would weaken her resolve to keep Sean at arm's length. She was too busy trying to earn that four thousand dollars before January to get involved in a relationship. Maybe in a few months, when things settled down, she could try again. But for now, she had her imagination and her vibrator and neither of them had ever lied to her.

"Is Sean coming over for dinner tonight?" Jonathan asked.

"Did you text him?" she snapped.

Her anger went right over his head. "No, but I will if you want to."

"If you touch my phone, you are grounded for life and I'll put security on your iPad so you have to do book reports before you can play your games."

"All right. All right," he groused.

He chewed his cereal while Liz reveled in the peace and quiet. The sleepy fog in her head started to clear by the end of her second cup. All night, her dreams were Cinderella bondage stories with her and Sean as the lead characters. She was going to wear out the batteries on her vibrator.

"When are we going to see Sean again?"

Liz was a little more ready for this conversation after the caffeine hit. "Sweetheart, Sean wasn't who he said he was. He was pretending to be something he wasn't."

"You always tell me that appearances don't count. It's what's inside that counts. Is Sean a bad guy?"

Sighing, Liz set down her coffee cup. "It's not that easy. No, he's not a bad guy. He's a pretty good guy."

"He just made a mistake, right? Aren't you always telling me that people make mistakes all the time? It's a part of growing up." Jonathan put his cereal bowl in the sink and was about to chug some of the almond milk from the carton.

At her upraised eyebrows, he explained. "I'm finishing up the last bit."

"Get a glass."

"But then we'll have to wash the glass," he protested.

Liz glared him down and he poured the last of the almond milk into a glass.

"Sean is already a grown up. He lied. He knew what he was doing wrong and he did it anyway."

"Did he say he was sorry?" Jonathan rinsed out the carton and folded the cardboard container so it fit into the recycle bin.

Liz's mouth opened. He did. He even begged for forgiveness. She nodded.

"Did you accept his apology?" Jonathan drank the milk in one long gulp.

She shook her head.

"Why not?"

Liz wanted to run away from the question or yell at him to go to his room. He was asking hard questions that she didn't have easy answers for. But she owed it to him to try and explain. "He hurt my feelings. Sometimes a sorry doesn't fix that. How can I trust someone will tell the truth when the friendship started with lies? Do you understand? What would you do if you found out Madison only liked you because you have *Angry Birds* on your iPad?"

"Mom, everyone has *Angry Birds*." Jonathan laughed at her.

"I know. But pretend. She became your friend just so you could play *Angry Birds* and then one day you find out that's why she approached you. How would you feel?"

Jonathan thought about it. "Did she still want to be my friend after I found out?"

"Yes," Liz said.

"Did we do other things than play *Angry Birds*, like take boxing lessons and have fun?"

"Sure." Liz took his dirty cup and washed it, rinsed it, and set it in the dish drainer to dry.

"I'd be mad. But if she was sorry and we still had fun together, isn't that what it's all about? Having a friend who cares about me and who I have a good time with? How we met shouldn't matter as long as she's not lying about staying my friend. Right?" He looked up at her with hopeful eyes.

"You are so damned smart." Liz hugged him to her. "I'm proud you're my son."

"So, can I take boxing lessons?" He peeked up at her, hope shining in his eyes.

"We'll see." She kissed the top of his head.

Con artist.

They had a ton of chores to do. Saturday was chore day. Sunday was fun day. Their least favorite of the chores was laundry. First, they had to haul all the dirty clothes down to the basement machines. Then wait for the washer and dryer. Then haul the clean clothes back up. They took a walk around the neighborhood and did some shopping during the cycles. When they were trudging up the stairs carrying the clean baskets, Liz noticed a thick manila envelope leaning against her door.

Not again.

"Look, Mom, someone left us a package."

Jonathan snagged it before she could set the laundry down and take it.

"Jonathan, wait. Don't open it."

But he had peeked inside already. Wrinkling his nose, he put it on top of her basket of clean clothes. "It's just paperwork."

She set up Jonathan with the task of putting his folded clothes away neatly. Liz dumped her basket on the floor and emptied the contents of the envelope out on her bedspread. There were college scholarship applications and pamphlets. Government grants and federal programs. Each one tailored for her. One was for single mothers. One was for cancer survivors. Yet another was for low-income families, and even more for self-employed women or women who owned their own businesses.

"Oh," Liz pressed a hand to her heart. She knew there were opportunities out there. She even searched for them, but she never gave them more than a cursory look. This large envelope was the narrowed-down version of all the sites and opportunities that had overwhelmed her.

Sarah wouldn't have done it. She would have written a check. Everyone else was too busy or wouldn't have thought of it. That left one person. A cynical part of her said that he'd do anything to get back in her good graces, and then the sensible part asked why would he want to unless he really did feel the same way whether he was an undergrad or a PhD candidate.

She picked up her phone and called him. She almost dropped it when a woman answered. Well, there went that idea. He went straight from her apartment and right to this woman. Liz gave a shaky laugh. While she was rubbing herself into a frenzy, Sean was probably having kinky sex with the woman on the other end of the phone. Maybe he didn't send over the applications. It was probably Peter, anyway.

Way to jump to conclusions, dummy.

"Hello?" the woman said again. "Is this Liz?"

Panicked, Liz almost dropped the phone, but then realized he probably had caller ID. "Um yes, I was looking for Sean, but I don't want to bother him. I'll just hang up."

Liz was about to press the hang-up button when she heard, "You won't bother him. He's unconscious."

✳✳✳ ✳✳✳

It galled Liz that the first time she was going to Sean's apartment, it wasn't because he invited her. In fact, the big dummy didn't even know she was on her way. Jonathan was pleased as punch to be spending his Saturday at the Cannings' place. Cole's video game setup looked like NASA, only with newer tech. Sarah only shook her head and demanded details—really good ones—after Jonathan went to bed.

The woman on Sean's phone turned out to be his sister's girlfriend. Laverne had just checked him out of the hospital and had tucked him into bed. From their brief conversation, she told Liz that Sean had had a sparring match in the gym this morning. Laverne had shown up to cheer him on and wound up seeing him take a lucky shot to the chin.

They called the paramedics when they couldn't rouse him. He came around before they got there, but was having a hard time with details.

Sean lived in Astoria Park, which was nowhere near NYU or the Silver Campus. It was close to McManus's gym and to the clinic where he worked. She had checked out Sabrina's story and discovered where Sean *really* worked when he wasn't teaching sociology classes.

Laverne let her in. "He's sleeping, but if you want, you can peek in on him."

"Sleeping? I thought you weren't supposed to let a concussed person sleep." Liz rushed into the bedroom Laverne indicated. She recognized the walls and background from their Skype conversations.

Sean was in bed, fully clothed. He had a cut under his eye and bruising under his jaw. Tiptoeing to his side, she pulled the sheet over him and kissed his forehead. He didn't stir. Liz closed the door behind her and leaned against it. Her knees were shaking.

"The doctors said it was okay for him to get some rest. He wasn't throwing up and his eyes were normal, not dilated." Laverne helped her to a chair at the kitchen table and got her a glass of water.

"What happened?" Liz said.

"He was doing really well. They were trading blows back and forth." Laverne did some boxing moves. "It was all new to me, but it wasn't a real match or anything. It was just practice."

"Practice?" Liz sputtered on her water. "He got sent to the hospital. He's all bruised and cut." She wanted to cry. She wanted to find the other fighter and kick his ass.

"It was just a bad punch. Kyle, his opponent, is so upset."

"He should be." Liz forced herself to take a drink of water and calm down. She looked around Sean's apartment. There were electronics and stacks of paper everywhere. The furniture looked brand new and definitely not garage-sale finds. He had art on his wall that showed off his style. They were seriolithographs and not posters, either. Now she knew why they never came back here. Location aside, even with a roommate, an undergraduate would have a hard time affording this place. It made her apartment look shabby.

Liz took a fortifying breath. "I'm glad you were there for him today."

"Me, too," she said, looking at her hands. "No one should have to face the hospital all alone."

A pang of sympathy went through her. "I'm so sorry for your loss."

Laverne's lip tilted up in a half smile. "Thanks."

"Sean talks about her with great love. I'm sorry I never met her."

"I miss her," Laverne's voice quivered. "Sometimes I feel like she's still alive and I'll walk in the door and she'll be there waiting for me. And when she's not, my heart breaks all over again, because I know she never will be. I'd give anything to have her back."

Of course Sean didn't have any tissues, but Liz found a roll of paper towels. She brought it back to the table and handed Laverne one.

"I'm all right," Laverne said. "I just go through these crying jags. Sean went crazy, and I cry at the drop of the hat. Grief. It's a funny thing."

"Yeah," Liz said.

"Can I ask you a question?" Laverne blew her nose.

Liz shrugged. "I guess."

"Do you love him? Because he is head over heels in love with you."

"I can't be in love with him," Liz said, shaking her head.

"Then why did you come over here so fast?" Laverne grabbed another paper towel and wet it at the kitchen sink. She folded it up over her eyes.

"I was worried. He's a friend." It sounded false to Liz's ears. She had come over because she was terrified.

Laverne eased her head back and pressed the cold damp paper towel to her eyelids. "Can I tell you something?"

Liz got up and put her glass in the sink. "Go ahead." She'd been schooled by her nine-year-old this morning, and now it looked like she was going to hear it from Sean's sister's lover, too.

"He wouldn't get in the ambulance until I promised him to deliver an envelope to you. He was afraid it was going to get lost. He wasn't sure if he would remember it or you. That's how fucked up he was after he got hit. Sean made me promise I would tell you that he would always love you—even if he never remembered it."

Laverne handed her the roll of paper towels. Liz barely heard the rest of it through her own crying jag. She was so sick of crying! But it was cathartic.

"Men do crazy shit all the time. I swear their brains aren't wired right. He's an ass. He's too intellectual sometimes and other times he's too physical. But he's a nice damn guy. Forgive him already. And if you can't, stop giving him hope."

Liz nodded. She had some decisions to make.

"I've got an appointment." Laverne tossed the paper towel in the garbage. "Will you be here until he wakes up?"

"Sure," Liz wanted to see him up and lucid before she went anywhere.

"If he's not up and you have to go, you call me and I'll come back." Laverne tossed her purse over her arm.

"I'll be here until morning."

"What about your kid?"

"He's staying at a friend's."

Laverne nodded and sighed, "Let me know if he takes a turn for the worse."

"Is that possible?" Liz had thought the worst was over.

"Head trauma is tricky. The doctor gave him some painkillers, and he may need them when he wakes up. You'll take care of him?"

"I will," Liz promised.

"Good, because he's my little brother now. Desiree will haunt me if I let anything bad happen to him." She cast a fond look at the bedroom door.

After Laverne left, Liz tidied up until she couldn't stand it anymore and went into the bedroom to hold Sean's hand while he slept.

Chapter Nineteen

*F*uck.

Goddamn Donovan.

Every inch of him ached. He wanted a shower and a beer. It felt like heavy bags were holding down his entire body. Getting up was too much effort. Sean just lay there and, as clarity came back, he became aware that someone was holding his hand.

Forcing his eyelids to raise, he saw Liz sitting there.

"Liz?" he tried to get up.

"Lie down," she said. "You were knocked out."

"You were there?" The details were still fuzzy.

"No, Laverne called me."

That was right. He remembered that.

"Did you get the scholarship applications?"

Liz bit her lip. "Yes, thank you."

He relaxed back into his pillow. "Good." He was sleepy.

"Can I get you anything?" she asked.

"You can get your sweet ass in bed with me," he mumbled. A far away thought pinged him that might not be the right thing to say, so he ignored it. She dropped his hand and the ping blossomed to a pain in his heart.

Oh right. She hates me.

But the next thing he registered was her warm body getting under the covers. He slung his arm around her and pulled her close.

"Love you," he said before sleep claimed him again.

✳✳✳ ✳✳✳

Sean was in the ring, fully suited up. The slight wine hangover from last night bothered him, but he drank enough water that he didn't think he'd be dehydrated. Jogging in place to stay loose, he watched McManus give Donovan some last-minute tips.

The scene flickered and he was ready to come out swinging. Turning around, Mary—no Desiree—was in the ring with him. She was wearing a Rockette outfit and practicing her kicks.

"Hi Squirt," she said. "Are you mad at me?"

"No." Sean knew this was a dream because his mouthguard was still in, but he was speaking perfectly. "But you're dead."

"And you're sleeping." Her costume changed to a tin soldier and she did the Christmas dance they saw every year at Radio City Music Hall.

"Why did you smoke that shit?" He swung at a giant crack pipe. It shattered into pieces of glass that tore into his face. He couldn't see through all the blood.

"I fucked up," she said.

"I fucked up, too." He danced around her, throwing punches at a fake opponent.

"You can still turn it around." Her kicks were getting higher and closer.

"Can I?"

"Tell Mom and Dad I love them." And then she high-kicked him in the chin.

✳✳✳ ✳✳✳

When he woke, his head was screaming and he had to take a piss. He made it to a sitting position before his gut roiled and the room spun.

The bed shifted as Liz sat up. "Do you need help?"

Nodding caused pain like ice picks jammed into his eyes and ears. "Yeah," he said quietly.

Fucking Donovan could hit.

Liz helped him to his feet and guided him to the bathroom.

"I got this," he said, eyes slits. "Just don't turn on any lights."

"Yell if you need help."

"I can take a piss by myself. I got hit in the head, not the dick," he growled.

She smacked him on the ass. "Be nice. I'm going to get you a glass of water so you can take your pain meds."

"You're an angel," he said and closed the bathroom door in her face.

He caught a glimpse of his face in the mirror and wished he hadn't. He had been in worse shape, but not for a while. Trying to remember the fight, Sean steadied himself on the bathroom counter. There must have been an angle he didn't count on. He thought he'd had Donovan's timing down.

The dizziness forced him to sit down to take care of his business. When he was done, he thought about a shower but didn't think he'd be able to stand that long. Maybe later after the meds kicked in. Liz was waiting for him with the glass and two horse pills.

Grimacing, Sean swallowed them down and allowed her to lead him back to bed. "I'm okay," he said.

"I can see that." She tucked him in and sat down on the bed next to him.

"Want to fool around?"

Liz smiled and touched his face.

He winced.

"How about I get you an ice pack for your face?"

"That sounds good, too."

He tried to prop up the pillows to sit up, but it was too much effort. Besides, his ceiling was very entertaining, but not as entertaining as the inside of his eyelids. He heard her come back into the room. The bed sank a bit when she resumed her seat by his chest. Gently, a damp dishcloth filled with ice touched his eye and cheekbone. He sighed at the cold relief.

"Thanks," he said, holding it in place. "Not that I'm complaining, but what are you doing here?" She was the last person he expected to see, let alone be in his bed. Part of him was wondering if he had dreamed that. Nah, if he had dreamed it, they both would have been naked.

"Laverne let me in. I called to thank you for the applications and then she told me about your concussion."

"How did you know it was me who sent the applications?" he rasped. He had been working on them ever since the day she threw him out of her apartment.

"They were meticulously researched." Liz tucked the sheet up to his chest.

A smile cracked his face. "That's the nicest thing you've ever said to me. Well, aside from 'Fuck me Sean, harder.'"

"You're determined to get hit again, aren't you?"

"It's the concussion. It makes me say crazy things."

"Are you lying to me again?" she asked.

"Maybe a bit," he admitted, moving the ice pack to the other side of his face.

"Well, cut that shit out. I'm not putting up with that anymore."

He was still trying to figure out if he was dreaming this, too. He was convinced if she was still wearing clothes, this was reality. Reaching out, he poked her to see if she felt real. The poke was more like a soft touch on her arm. He removed the ice pack entirely so he could look at her with both eyes. Hope fluttered in his chest and he was worried that his head was still too fuzzy, but it sounded like she wasn't as done with him as she'd been before.

"So am I forgiven?"

It seemed like forever before she answered him.

"I'm getting there. I want to start over. This time, no lies."

"Deal," he said. Damn it, if he was dreaming, he didn't want to wake up.

She put the ice pack over his face. "Let the medication help you. We've got all the time in the world."

Chapter Twenty

Sean recovered over the next few weeks. Liz was happy to see that there weren't any side effects from the fight other than slowing him down. She held firm to them getting to know each other as if it were from the beginning.

"I mean it," she told him. "Start with 'I saw your Facebook post' and go from there."

They traded texts and graduated to Skyping every day. No hanky-panky. Although, late one night, she "accidentally" called him while she had her vibrator out.

He watched her perform without saying a word. But the next week, wouldn't you know it, he "accidentally" called her while he was jerking off.

It was an interesting twist, but it gave them both time to do things right this time. Because she was upfront about Jonathan, they had their first date, the three of them together, at the Bronx Zoo. After that, they included him on a date night once a week for dinner. Jonathan was thrilled because that meant he could have bacon on his pizza.

Liz was less than thrilled about that, but it made him happy, and as long as she didn't have to eat it too, she could deal. Jonathan made sure to give them "alone time," but Liz kept Sean to just a hug and a kiss. She was adamant about going slow this time. So what if she had to buy a few packs of double A batteries?

By mid-November, Sean persuaded her into French kisses and dry humping on the couch—not that she needed much persuasion. And if she accidentally forgot to wear underwear . . . oops.

Thanksgiving rolled around and everybody was invited to Liz's apartment.

"Let me get this straight," Sarah asked on a late-night phone call. "You're going to introduce us to Sean, like we've never met him before."

"That's right," Liz said, brushing flour from her forehead. She was baking the rolls the night before so it was one less thing she had to do tomorrow. "We've started over."

"You have issues." Sarah laughed. "What am I supposed to bring again?"

Liz almost dropped the phone. The stores were probably all out. What was she going to do?

"Just kidding. The yams are cooking away. And before you go and harass anyone else, Holly and Marc have the fruit and quinoa salad; Peter and Pol are bringing the artichokes; and Brian was bringing the pies—I double checked, they're vegan."

Liz let out a huge sigh. "Don't do that to me."

"What's Mr. Perfect—I mean the sexy stranger I've yet to meet— bringing?" Sarah moved the phone away, but Liz still heard her say, "Cole, the baby needs to get changed. Can you do that? I'm on the phone."

"Nice excuse," Liz chortled.

"Any port in a storm."

"Sean's bringing a fruit platter and his sister-in-law, Laverne, is bringing wine."

"I like her already," Sarah said.

Dinner went well. Liz was lucky to have such good friends. Not only did they eat her tofurkey, but everyone pretended this was the first time they had met Sean. It helped that Brian left Sabrina home. Liz wasn't quite ready to forgive *her* yet.

Sarah gave Liz an early Christmas present, subsidizing the amount of the nipple tattooing that her insurance didn't cover.

"I don't know how I can ever thank you," Liz said, her eyes and nose filling up.

"Just don't put them on the Christmas cards," Sarah joked.

She even went to the plastic surgeon's office with her. For a moment, Liz had a flashback to the cancer treatments. Sarah had been there for her then, too.

The procedure didn't take as long as she thought it would. Liz marveled at the results. Now, when she looked in the mirror, Liz saw a familiar body. Instead of the lifeless lumps, her breasts almost looked perky. She should have done this right away, but she hadn't been ready for it. Liz remembered she didn't think she'd ever show them to anyone again, so who cared. It was a marvel that she was ready for Sean to see them, scars and all.

And at almost the last minute to register for the January semester, Liz's new scholarship came through. It was just for the one class, but it was a start. She was able to start pursuing her dream after all.

"We're going to go see the Rockettes to celebrate," Sean said and arranged for Jonathan and her to go with him to Radio City Music Hall to see the Christmas show. They went during the week. No need to wrestle with the weekend crowds.

Then they headed over to Rockefeller Center to get their picture taken next to the angels blowing horns. Liz held his hand and started to feel pieces of her life clicking together. After ice skating, they ate roasted chestnuts from a street vendor and drank hot chocolate. And, of course, before going home, Jonathan conned them into hitting the

Lego Store. Sean kept him busy building a few mini figs while Liz arranged to have a package shipped to her.

Before she could blink, Christmas Eve came. Liz made a special dinner for just the three of them. After dinner, they went caroling and came back to put the finishing touches on the tree. Jonathan and Sean ate their weight in popcorn, but the garland still looked all right.

Jonathan was fast asleep by ten. After Liz checked on him, she opened the door to her bedroom and crooked her finger at Sean. If she had anything to say about it, they'd be opening up more than their presents.

"I have a surprise for you," Sean said, kissing her.

She unbuckled his pants. "I bet I know what it is."

"Wait," he said. "I want to do something for you."

Liz quivered. "Anything."

"Be right back."

Being left alone in her bedroom on Christmas Eve was not what she had in mind. Did she put him off too many times? Was she too subtle about tonight? Damn it, she was going to get laid. Liz was about to chase after him when he shouldered into the room. He was carrying a kitchen chair and two large shopping bags.

"What's all this?"

He closed the door and locked it. "It's your Christmas gift."

That's what I'm talking about.

Setting the chair against the closed door, Sean pointed. "Sit here please."

"Well, since you asked so nice," she said and sat.

"Do you trust me?"

"Sure." Liz arched a look at him.

He dangled a pair of handcuffs in front of her.

Oh my.

"Can I cuff you to the chair?"

Words failed her so she could only nod. He cuffed her hands behind her back through the chair's slats so she couldn't move.

The blindfold came next. Liz's panties were already soaked and he hadn't even done anything yet.

"Can you see?" he asked.

"No."

"Can you get your hands free?"

"No. Do I need a safe word?"

"Just say stop or no, that'll work." Sean kissed her, flipping up her skirt and fondling her thighs. Then he moved away just when things were starting to get good. She heard him rustling around, getting undressed. She wondered what he was up to. Liz let her imagination go wild. Would he put his cock in her mouth while she was helpless to stop him? That made her writhe on the chair until she realized that position would be too awkward to be fun.

More rustling and she wondered what was taking so long. Just come over her and touch me, she wanted to scream. Liz didn't mind being handcuffed to the chair, but the blindfold was starting to annoy her. "Are you almost ready?"

What was he doing anyway?

"Patience," Sean chided.

After a few more moments, the only clue was the clack of keyboard keys.

"You better not be turning on a webcam," she warned.

"Trust," he said in the same scolding tone.

A seductive beat full of drum and bass rolled across her senses as music started to play, soft enough that it wouldn't wake Jonathan.

The blindfold came off.

"What?" she managed.

Sean was dressed in a tuxedo.

"Nice."

He started to strip, starting with the jacket. His hips undulated to the beat as the coat fell to the ground. The shirt was next, button by button. Each beat and drive of the music revealing Sean's hard, muscled chest and stomach.

Liz's mouth was dry. Her pulse was pounding with the music and she could feel the bass on her clit.

Then he revealed the V on the planes of his hips as he opened his pants, sliding the zipper down. He wasn't wearing underwear.

"I'm all out of dollar bills." Her voice caught on the last word when he let his pants fall and stepped out of them.

"I've got no place to put them." Sean stalked toward her chair.

His cock was erect, thick to bursting. She hadn't seen it in a while. Liz pulled on her handcuffs. She wanted to be free to touch him. He straddled her on the chair and gave her a lap dance that teased her into biting his arm. Brushing his abs in her face, she could feel the hot, velvet length of his cock. He backed off and continued the dance. Head thrown back, Sean pantomimed fucking her. The head of his cock glistening with wetness showed her he wanted her, too. As the song ended, he turned away from her and danced the last few beats to show off his back and ass.

"Still think I wasn't a stripper?" he challenged.

"Uncuff me," she said, not recognizing the hungry voice as hers.

"You don't want to watch me play with myself?" He stroked his hand down his chest and grabbed his cock. "I've been doing a lot of this lately."

"I can help with that," she breathed, straining at the cuffs.

"I didn't want to presume," he said, still pumping his cock.

Liz's toes curled as she watched, riveted. He was the sexiest thing she had ever seen. "Sean, uncuff me."

"I will," he said. "But my hands are full right now." Coming closer, Sean knelt at her feet. He pushed her skirt all the way to her waist with one hand, all the while fisting his cock. She spread her thighs.

"Yeah," he grunted. "Show me that pretty pussy of yours."

Liz rattled her cuffs. "Please. I'll do anything."

"Will you let me take off your panties?"

"Yes," she moaned.

He peeled them off her. Pulling her down on the seat with a rough tug, he spread her legs wide. Sean looked his fill.

"Can I lick you?"

"Yes," she panted.

Flicking his tongue from back to front, Sean moaned. "I missed how you taste."

"More," Liz said.

"Not just yet." He stood up, rubbing himself again. She tried to hook him with her ankles, to draw him closer, but he was just out of reach.

"Did you want something?" He came around to her side, brushed the head of his cock over her cheek.

Turning her head, she opened her mouth. He let her suck on the head. To hell with the angle being awkward.

"Oh, your tongue should be a lethal weapon," he said, his voice deep from desire.

Liz wanted more. She bobbed her head and he stepped closer.

"Do you know what it does to me to see you sucking my cock while you're handcuffed and that wet pussy is mine for the taking?"

She slipped him out of her mouth. "So take it."

He took a step back and resumed jerking off. "Are you sure?"

"You weren't the only one dreaming of Christmas orgasms. Santa may only come once a year, but you and I are going to enjoy each other year-round." Liz licked her lips. "I liked the taste of you in my mouth," she purred. "Bring it back so I can suck it down my throat."

"Coming," he told her. "Don't look away."

As if she could. He erupted, spurting over his chest and stomach. Nostrils flared, Sean grunted like an animal, his whole body shaking.

"Now," he said. "I'll uncuff you."

Liz was tearing off her clothes one handed after he freed one wrist, not waiting while he opened the other handcuff. He helped her, stopping only when he realized she was taking off her bra.

"Are you sure?" he said.

"Get on that bed, O'Malley."

He did what he was told. The frenzy was riding her and she stripped completely. Not giving him a chance to react, she straddled his face. Sean reached up to hold her hips as she undulated on his mouth and tongue.

Sean knew just where to lick. Liz leaned back so she could feel the rasp of his whiskers against her inner thighs. He clamped her close, growling into her pussy. The vibrations tickled like the bass line. Stars exploded under her eyelids and her orgasm shook her apart.

Liz thought she blacked out for a second because in the next moment, she was flat on her back. Her legs wrapped around Sean's waist as he drove into her.

"Yes," she cried out, forgetting to keep her voice down.

Sean's mouth covered hers as she continued to cry out her pleasure. His body was relentless. Thrusting hard, deep, and fast, Sean's thick cock filled her over and over again. He was like a machine and soon she was writhing, needing more. Needing him. She came again. Liz's fingers dug half-moons into his shoulders. His mouth absorbed her screams of pleasure, grinding until their teeth clacked. She went limp, enjoying the push of his body into hers while he finished in a shuddering mass of moans.

Not done by a long shot, they rubbed each other's bodies. He poured coconut oil over her and it didn't even occur to Liz that she was rubbing her breasts over his chest until the oil he poured over them dried. As Sean reached for the bottle of oil again, she straddled him. His cock fit inside her like it belonged there. She sighed, taking the bottle away from him. Squeezing her inner muscles, Liz rocked a bit on his cock. When she had his full attention, she squirted oil over her breasts and began to massage it in. She felt him swell inside her. Loving the rapt attention on his face, she acted as though she could feel herself tugging on her nipples. Hefting her breasts, she offered them to him, but he was too transfixed to do anything but sigh her name. Taking his hands, Liz placed them on her chest and encouraged him to stroke them. She rode him hard.

It was thrilling to take a man like this again. Watch his lust-soaked face as he lavished attention on her body. It was getting her off.

"You are the most beautiful woman I have ever seen," he said. "I will never get tired of telling you that."

"I won't get tired of hearing it," she said, leaning down to kiss him.

She bounced rough on him, needing to feel him penetrate deep. When she came, her muscles contracted so tight that he cried out. Liz kept it up until she squeezed another orgasm out of him.

Cuddled up next to him, she played with his balls while he tried to get his breath back. "I'm making up for lost time," Liz purred in his ear and nibbled on it.

"You're going to give me a heart attack," he told her.

"I loved it when you danced for me."

Pulling her on top of him, Sean poured more oil on her back and massaged it in.

"You are so damn sexy," she murmured in his ear when he soothed a sore muscle.

Turning her over, he nestled his cock in the curve of her ass and repeated the oil down her front. Pausing to rub her clit, Sean sucked on her neck while the other hand held her in place by clamping on her breast.

Liz felt loved, owned, and thoroughly decadent.

"I love you," she keened when his fingers wouldn't stop until she crested. Her whole body jolted as if she was connected to a live wire. "I love you," she sobbed out again.

"Mine," he claimed, turning her again so he could kiss her lips.

The night went on like that until all the coconut oil was gone and their bodies were exhausted and sore. The sheets would never be the same either.

"Merry Christmas," he said in her ear as their caresses grew more lazy and loving.

"Did you get everything you wanted for Christmas?" she asked.

"Not yet. I'll get your ass later." He tickled his finger over that little area.

Wrapping her legs around his, Liz sighed in contentment. "I might even wake up for that."

Epilogue

Sarah and Cole were hosting a New Year's Eve ball at the Ritz Carlton. Jonathan convinced them to make it a costume party. He was a yellow minion complete with fart gun, thanks to Sean. He fell asleep in a Queen Anne's chair that was older than most of the party-goers. Sean carried him up to their suite and Mrs. Ritter, dressed as Mary Poppins, was pleased to call it a night and watch over him.

Peter and Pol went as Sherlock Holmes and Watson. They planned an elaborate murder mystery for the guests to figure out. Honey and Marc came as Holly Golightly and George Peppard's characters from *A Breakfast at Tiffany's*, although Marc looked more like Hannibal from the A-team. Liz thought it must be the cigar. Brian was there solo, as Sabrina was finally in rehab. He was hoping she'd pull herself together, but the last he heard, she was offering blow jobs for uppers. He was dressed as Frankenstein and was content to eat all the marzipan cookies in sight.

And, of course, Liz convinced Sean to wear his Prince Charming costume again. She had plans on how the night was going to end after all the champagne was gone. And it didn't come close to how Disney ended the movie.

They wandered through the hotel looking for Peter's next clue.

"This way," Sean said, dragging her behind a large potted plant.

"I'm stumped," Liz said. "I think I need more champagne."

"I need more you," he growled and thrilled her by pushing her up against the wall.

"Why Prince Charming, what ever are you going to do to me?" Liz fluttered her eyes closed and waited for the kiss that would melt her garter belt off. But it didn't come. She opened her eyes, just as he was dropping to his knees.

"Sean, not here," she whispered, scandalized.

Yes, here!

But instead of crawling under her skirt, he pressed play on his iPod. "A Dream is a Wish Your Heart Makes" started up. He set the iPod on the rim of the plant.

"What are you up to?" she asked, looking around to see how private they were.

He reached into his jacket pocket and held up a ring box.

"Liz Carter, you would make me the happiest man in the world if you would be my princess. Marry me?"

Don't start blubbering.

"I asked Jonathan," Sean said. "And he gave me two thumbs up."

"Two thumbs?" Liz's lips quivered. "That's quite an endorsement."

Taking the ring out of the box, he slipped it on her finger. She counted three lovely round diamonds.

"That represents me, you, and Jonathan," he said.

"Yes," Liz said, tears dripping down her cheeks. "Of course I'll marry you."

He shot to his feet and whirled her around. And then she got the kiss she had been waiting for.

Publisher's Note

Breast cancer is the second leading cause of cancer death in American women. The American Cancer Society reports that about 1 in 8 women in the United States (12%) will develop breast cancer during their lifetime.

Forty thousand women will die from breast cancer this year.

According to the National Cancer Institute, "When breast cancer is detected early, in the localized stage, the five year survival rate is 98%."

Early detection is key to stopping the cancer's spread.

• Schedule monthly breast self-exams. An easy way to remember to do your exam is do it every month on your day of birth. For example, if you were born on June 16, conduct a thorough self-examination on the sixteenth day of every month.

• Get a yearly mammogram if you are forty years old or older.

• Get a clinical breast exam by a health-care professional yearly if you are forty or older, and at least once every three years if you are in your twenties and thirties.

For more information about early detection, see the American Cancer Society's website at Cancer.org, and to connect with other breast cancer survivors online or for support, check out Pink-Link.org.

FICTION JAMESON

Jameson, Jenna.
Spice

SEAST
R4001817395

SOUTHEAST
Atlanta-Fulton Public Library